2030

Resisting the New World Order

Written by:
Alan E Shields

INDEX

Introduction

Dystopian World Setting

Backdrop: The Year 2030

The scene opens in a bustling city square, the skyline dominated by digital billboards flashing with vibrant propaganda. It's 2030, a year that once symbolized hope and futuristic splendor but now stands as a testament to a world reshaped, not by the hands of its people, but by the meticulous designs of global powerhouses - the United Nations, the World Economic Forum, and their powerful elite friends.

In a small, cramped café, a group of individuals huddle over steaming cups of synthetic coffee. The café, like everything else, is a blend of the old world charm and the new digital order.

Mara, a sharp-tongued waitress with a hidden intellect, quips to her regular customer, Tom, as she refills his cup: "Enjoying the taste of progress, Tom? They say it's brewed with 50% efficiency and 50% surveillance."

Tom, a middle-aged man with a knack for sarcasm, smirks in response, "Ah, nothing wakes you up in the morning like a good old dose of dystopian dread, right Mara?"

The digital billboard outside flickers, showcasing a world of unity and prosperity under the U.N. and WEF initiatives. Gleaming cities, happy faces, and slogans like 'One World, One People' dominate the screen.

Mara rolls her eyes: "If they cram any more happiness into those ads, I might just burst into tears."

Tom chuckles: "Now, now, tears are probably rationed too. Better save them for something worthwhile."

Their banter is a common scene, a way for the common folk to cope with the overbearing new reality. People like Mara and Tom have adapted to the new world with a blend of humor and resignation. They represent the average citizen, those who have seen the world morph into a digital empire of control.

As the billboard displays a grand image of a U.N. meeting, a young man at a nearby table, Alex, a recent university graduate and an idealist at heart, speaks up. "You know, they promised us a future of technological wonders. I just didn't expect those wonders to be used to count my every step and monitor my every word."

Mara turns to Alex, her expression softening, "That's the trouble with promises, Alex. They're like the fine print on a contract – always twisted to fit the one holding the pen."

The café, a microcosm of the world outside, is filled with a diverse group of individuals, each trying to find their place in this new order. The atmosphere is a mix of nostalgia for the past and a begrudging acceptance of the present.

The city outside the café window bustles with activity. Autonomous vehicles glide silently down the streets, their passengers' eyes fixed on personal screens. Drones hover above, some carrying advertisements, others – more sinister in nature – equipped with cameras, perpetually watching.

This is the world of 2030. A world where ambition and controversy have collided to create a society that is at once advanced and regressive, free and imprisoned, hopeful and despondent. It is within this world that our story unfolds, a narrative that explores the depths of human resilience and the enduring quest for freedom in an age of unyielding control.

Global Shift: The Emergence of Centralized Governance

In a corner of the same café, overshadowed by the gleaming skyscrapers adorned with digital banners proclaiming unity and progress, sits a group of old-timers. They're engaged in a heated discussion, their voices a mixture of nostalgia and disbelief.

Old Man Jenkins, a retired history teacher, shakes his head: "I remember just a few years ago when the world was a patchwork of countries, each with its own flag and anthem. Now, it's like we're living in a giant corporation, and the CEO is some global council."

Ms. Rivera, a former journalist with a keen eye, adds: "It's all branding, Jenkins. Countries were out, 'Global Sectors' are in. It's efficient, uniform... soulless."

Jenkins scoffs: "Efficient? Ha! They can't even decide on which universal language to use in their meetings. Last I heard, it was a toss-up between Esperanto and Corporate Jargon."

Laughter erupts from the table, a brief respite from the weight of their conversation. These conversations are a testament to the seismic shifts that have occurred. The dissolution of national boundaries didn't just redraw maps; it redefined identities. People like Jenkins and Ms. Rivera feel like relics of a bygone era, struggling to find their place in this new world order.

Outside the café, giant screens display a live feed from the Global Governance Assembly, a sleek and sterile environment where representatives, more like polished celebrities than politicians, debate policies that affect billions. The Assembly, a symbol of this new era, stands as a stark contrast to the disheveled charm of the café and its patrons.

A young tech worker, overhearing the old-timers, interjects: "You know, I heard they use algorithms now to make decisions. They say it's impartial, free from human bias."

Ms. Rivera smirks: "Ah, yes, because nothing says 'human touch' like a decision made by a machine."

The café erupts into a mixture of chuckles and contemplative silence. The irony isn't lost on anyone. In this new era of extreme globalization, where decisions are made by distant, faceless entities and enforced by an intricate web of technology, the concept of human touch has become an antiquated notion.

As the day progresses, the café serves as a sanctuary for diverse voices and opinions, a place where the remnants of the old world collide with the stark realities of the new. It's in these conversations, filled with humor and sarcasm, that the true impact of this global shift is felt - in the lives of those who reminisce about the past and those who are trying to navigate the complexities of the present. This is the world in 2030: interconnected, governed from afar, and yet still clinging to the fragments of what once was.

Technological Transformation: The Digital Revolution

The café, with its quaint charm, stands in sharp contrast to the technological wonders that pervade the city. At a nearby table, a young couple is engaged in a conversation that captures the essence of this new era.

Sara, a tech-savvy university student, waves her Digital ID in front of a scanner to pay for their coffee: "You know, I can't remember the last time I used actual cash. With this ID, it's like my whole life is in one place — convenient but kind of creepy."

Mark, her companion, a bit of a skeptic, replies: "Convenient until it decides you've had too much caffeine for the day and cuts you off. Then what? Barter with your old vinyl collection?"

Their laughter is a mix of humor and underlying concern. The implementation of Digital IDs and CBDCs has streamlined financial transactions to mere gestures and taps. Yet, beneath this veneer of efficiency lies a more unsettling reality – the gradual erosion of privacy and autonomy.

In another part of the café, a middle-aged man named Greg, who lost his job to automation, speaks to his friend, Lila, a bank employee adjusting to the new digital currency system.

Greg, with a hint of bitterness: "Remember when we used to have wallets filled with different currencies from our travels? Now, it's all just numbers on a screen. Feels like we lost a bit of the world's color."

Lila, trying to be optimistic, responds: "At least we don't have to deal with exchange rates anymore. And hey, no more waiting in line at the bank!"

Greg smirks: "Yeah, because nothing screams 'human connection' like talking to a chatbot about your financial woes."

Their exchange highlights the mixed feelings about the technological transformation that has swept through society. For some, like Sara, it's a marvel of convenience. For others, like Greg, it's a reminder of what has been lost in the relentless march of progress.

Outside, the city is a symphony of digital interaction. People glide through automated doors, purchase items with a simple scan of their ID, and interact with holographic interfaces that float in the air. Yet, in the eyes of the café's patrons, these advancements seem to have come at a cost – a world where every transaction is tracked, every movement monitored, and every aspect of identity digitized.

This technological transformation, while celebrated by many, has fundamentally altered the nature of personal identity and financial transactions, creating a society that is hyper-connected yet paradoxically disconnected from the human essence of its past. The café, in its small rebellion against the digital tide, remains a haven for those seeking a reminder of a less complicated world.

Social Credit System: The All-Seeing Eye

The café's retro charm provides a stark contrast to the pervasive atmosphere of surveillance outside. At a small, somewhat isolated table, a lively discussion unfolds among a group of young adults, their conversation tinged with both humor and a hint of fear.

Kevin, a graphic designer with a rebellious streak, chuckles: "So, I sneezed without covering my mouth yesterday, and my Social Credit Score dropped by five points. At this rate, I'll be banned from public transport for catching a cold."

Jenna, a nurse with a dry wit, responds: "Better stock up on those vitamins, Kevin. Wouldn't want you walking to work in the rain, now would we?"

Their banter masks the underlying unease they feel about the Social Credit Score System. This omnipresent system monitors and evaluates every aspect of individual behavior, linking it to societal privileges or restrictions. It's a digital leash, invisible yet ever-tightening.

In another corner, an elderly man named Mr. Dawson, reminisces to his grandchild about the days before the system was implemented.

Mr. Dawson, with a nostalgic sigh: "Back in my day, we were free to make mistakes. Now, it seems like every little thing you do is being watched and judged."

His grandchild, Lily, a teenager born into this new world, asks curiously: "But Grandpa, doesn't the system make everything safer and more organized?"

Mr. Dawson replies: "Perhaps, Lily, but at what cost? We traded our freedom for the illusion of security. Now, we're just numbers in a system, our worth determined by some algorithm."

Their exchange highlights the generational divide in perceptions of the Social Credit System. To Lily, it's a normal part of life, a tool for organization and safety. To Mr. Dawson, it represents a loss of personal freedom, a sentiment echoed by many in the café.

As the day progresses, customers come and go, their scores subtly influencing their interactions. A man gets denied his favorite table due to a recent dip in his score, while a woman receives a complimentary dessert for her high rating.

The Social Credit System has woven itself into the fabric of society, dictating access to services, shaping social interactions, and even altering personal relationships. It's a world where behavior is constantly measured, and conformity is rewarded, while individuality becomes a liability.

In this café, a rare haven from the all-seeing eye of the system, people find a space to breathe, to express themselves more freely, and to remember a time when their actions were their own. The contrast between the café's warmth and the cold efficiency of the outside world serves as a poignant reminder of what has been lost in the pursuit of order and control.

Introduction of Central Themes

Control and Surveillance: The Omnipresent Gaze

The café, a quaint relic in the heart of the city, buzzes with the energy of its patrons, each one a story in themselves, yet bound by the common thread of living under the unblinking eye of global governance.

At a table by the window, a group of office workers share hushed conversations, their tones tinged with a blend of humor and cynicism.

Rob, a middle-aged accountant with a penchant for dry humor, whispers: "I told my smart fridge I was on a diet, and now my Health Score is up. Who knew an appliance could be so judgmental?"

Nina, his colleague, a young marketing executive, laughs quietly: "At least your fridge cares. My smart watch docked points for not smiling enough at a staff meeting. Apparently, my 'corporate enthusiasm' needs work."

Their banter, light on the surface, reveals a deeper unease about the extent of surveillance they live under – where even household appliances and personal devices are part of the vast network monitoring their every move, behavior, and emotion.

In a secluded corner, an elderly man named Harold, once a professor of political science, engages in a more somber dialogue with his former student, Maya.

Harold, his voice tinged with regret: "We thought technology would liberate us, give us more freedom. But all it's done is forge new chains. We're freer to consume, yet more confined in thought and deed."

Maya, a young journalist, nods thoughtfully: "It's ironic, isn't it? In trying to connect the world, we've ended up more isolated, more scrutinized than ever."

Their conversation touches upon the heart of the story's central themes – the pervasive surveillance and the erosion of individual freedoms. In this new world order, every action is monitored, every choice analyzed, and personal agency seems like a relic of the past.

Across the café, a group of teenagers, the digital natives of this era, engage in a lively debate.

Tom, an outspoken member of the group, exclaims: "They say it's for our safety, for efficiency. But what's the point if we can't even make a joke without worrying about our Social Score?"

Leah, his friend, adds sarcastically: "Yeah, welcome to the age of 'Big Brother', where he's not just watching, he's also judging, scoring, and punishing."

Their conversation, laden with sarcasm, highlights the generational impact of this surveillance state. Despite growing up in this era of control, these young minds grapple with the implications on their identity and freedom.

This scene in the café, a microcosm of the larger society, sets the stage for the exploration of these themes. The narrative will delve into the lives of these characters, each affected in different ways by the overreaching control of global governance, weaving a tale that is both a reflection and a warning of a world where privacy is a myth, and freedom is a commodity.

Resistance and Hope: The Unyielding Flame

In the same café, where the air hums with the tension of a world under the thumb of omnipresent control, a different kind of conversation brews at a tucked-away table. Here, a small group of individuals, each carrying the spark of resistance, discuss their subtle acts of defiance.

Mia, a former librarian turned underground educator, shares in a low but passionate tone: "They can monitor our every move, but they can't police our thoughts. Not yet, anyway. Every banned book I distribute is a seed of freedom."

Carlos, a wry-humored street artist whose murals have become symbols of subtle dissent, adds: "And every piece of art I leave in the city's shadows is a whisper that not all of us have forgotten what it means to dream."

Their dialogue, a blend of defiance and hope, is a testament to the resilience of the human spirit. Even in a world that seeks to curtail every aspect of individuality, there are those who refuse to be fully tamed.

At another table, a group of teenagers, including Lily, Mr. Dawson's grandchild, animatedly discuss a secret project.

Lily, her eyes alight with a mix of mischief and determination, says: "We're working on an anonymous forum. A place online where people can speak freely, even if it's just to rant about their Social Score."

Her friend Jamal, a budding tech whiz, chimes in: "Yeah, and we're using old-school encryption methods. Let's see how they like a taste of their own medicine!"

Their enthusiasm and innovative spirit in finding ways to circumvent the system offer a glimpse of hope and a reminder that the desire for autonomy and freedom can never be fully extinguished.

In these interactions, the café becomes more than just a haven from the ever-watching eyes of the state; it becomes a breeding ground for resistance, a place where ideas are born and nurtured, where the flickering flame of hope is carefully shielded against the winds of oppression.

This narrative of resistance and hope runs parallel to the themes of control and surveillance. It poses profound questions about the nature of freedom and autonomy. What does it mean to be free in a world where your every move is watched? How does one hold onto hope when autonomy is but a distant memory?

As the story unfolds, these questions will be explored through the lives of these characters – Mia's quiet rebellion through knowledge, Carlos's defiant art, and the ingenuity of Lily and Jamal. Their stories, interwoven with those of others in the café, will paint a picture of a world on the brink – where the forces of control and surveillance are met with the enduring resilience and hope of the human spirit.

Consequences of Global Policies: The Tangled Web

In the heart of the café, where the aroma of coffee blends with the undercurrents of rebellion, a group of diverse patrons gathers, each one a living story of the consequences wrought by the global elite's policies.

Elena, a small business owner whose shop was replaced by a corporate chain, laments in a tone mixed with sorrow and bitterness: "They said it was for economic progress. But what progress is there when it's their pockets that get lined, and we're left with scraps?"

Beside her, Martin, a once-thriving farmer now turned city dweller, adds with a hardened edge to his voice: "Oh, they're great with their promises. 'Sustainable farming,' they said. And now? My fields are just data points on their fancy climate charts."

Their exchange paints a vivid picture of the everyday impact of global policies, where the lofty ideals of progress and sustainability often mask a grim reality of disenfranchisement and loss.

Across the room, a group of former factory workers, who lost their jobs to automation, share their stories.

Dave, a former technician, says with a wry chuckle: "They replaced me with a robot. Said it was more efficient. Funny, I don't recall efficiency helping me pay the bills."

His friend, Lisa, nods in agreement, adding: "And the best part? Now they want us to be 'retrained' for the digital economy. At our age, it's like teaching an old dog not only new tricks but how to code them too!"

Their conversations, while laced with humor, are a testament to the profound disconnect between the policies crafted in high-rise conference rooms and the reality on the ground. It's a world where the human element is often reduced to mere statistics and economic models.

Near the entrance, a young nurse named Rebecca speaks with an elderly patient, Mr. Thompson.

Rebecca, her voice a mix of compassion and frustration, explains: "I'm sorry, Mr. Thompson, but your health plan doesn't cover this anymore. The new global health policy prioritizes younger patients."

Mr. Thompson, a hint of despair in his eyes, responds: "So, my years don't just give me wisdom; they also make me a liability, huh? What a world we live in."

Their interaction sheds light on the more insidious aspects of these global policies — the cold calculus that values efficiency and cost-cutting over individual lives and stories.

As the day wanes and the café empties, these voices linger, echoing the far-reaching consequences of decisions made by a detached elite. Their stories intertwine to form a tapestry of a society grappling with the realities of global governance — a world where the everyday lives of ordinary people are often an afterthought in the grand scheme of progress and innovation.

Th s narrative thread, exploring the consequences of global policies, serves as a critical examination of the impact on the fabric of society. It de ves into the lives disrupted, dreams deferred, and voices silenced in the name of global efficiency and order. Through these personal stories, the novel not only critiques these policies but also highlights the resilience and adaptability of those who bear their weight.

Protagonist's Introduction:

Average Citizen: The Unseen Spark

In the subdued ambiance of the café, amidst the myriad of voices and undercurrents of dissent, we are introduced to our protagonist, Sam, an average citizen whose life epitomizes the mundane routine of existence in this controlled world.

Sam, a data analyst by profession, sits alone at a corner table, his eyes fixed on a small screen, scrolling through endless rows of data - a daily ritual that embodies his unremarkable life. He's the everyman, invisible in a sea of faces, adhering to the rhythms set by a world obsessed with control and surveillance.

Enter Jenna, Sam's childhood friend, who slides into the seat opposite him, her expression a mix of amusement and concern: "Still trying to find the meaning of life in those spreadsheets, Sam?"

Sam, without looking up, responds with a dry chuckle: "Oh, absolutely. I'm just about to crack the code to eternal happiness right after I finish analyzing these user engagement metrics."

Their banter, a blend of sarcasm and genuine affection, highlights Sam's underplayed wit and the comfortable familiarity of old friendships. Jenna, a nurse we met earlier, provides a contrast to Sam's introverted demeanor - she's outspoken, lively, and often serves as Sam's connection to the world beyond his data.

As they talk, Sam's gaze occasionally drifts to the window, to the world outside that moves with a precision and uniformity that he finds both reassuring and suffocating.

Jenna, following his gaze, says playfully: "Planning your great escape, are we? Last I checked, the wild beyond doesn't accept data reports as currency."

Sam, with a wistful smile, replies: "Maybe not, but at least out there, a man is more than just his Social Credit Score and work output."

This exchange lays the groundwork for Sam's character - a man of quiet intelligence, trapped in the mundanity of a life dictated by systems and numbers, yearning for something more, something real.

As they continue their conversation, discussing the trivialities of their day, there's a subtle shift in Sam's demeanor. The jokes and laughter don't quite reach his eyes, hinting at a deeper sense of discontent and a longing for change.

Little does Sam know, his unremarkable life is on the cusp of a dramatic turn. The seeds of dissent, sown in casual conversations and the hidden corners of his thoughts, are about to sprout, propelling him into a world far removed from the comfort of data and numbers.

In Sam, we find not just a character but a representation of the silent many in this dystopian world - those who, beneath the veneer of conformity, harbor the potential for resistance and change. His journey, though yet to unfold, is set against the backdrop of a society on the brink, where the push for control is met with the innate human desire for freedom and autonomy.

Initial Perspective: The Dawning Realization

As Sam, our protagonist, continues his usual routine, the initial acceptance of the new world order, a sentiment shared by many average citizens, begins to show cracks. The café, a familiar and comfortable spot, serves as the stage for this gradual awakening.

Jenna, noticing a hint of weariness in Sam's eyes, probes gently: "You've been looking more like one of your spreadsheets lately, Sam. Everything alright?"

Sam, stirring his coffee absentmindedly, replies: "It's just... have you ever wondered if all this – the scores, the constant monitoring – is really for our benefit? Or is it just another way to keep us in line?"

The question hangs in the air, a stark deviation from their usual light-hearted banter. Jenna, used to Sam's typically complacent nature, looks at him with a new interest.

Jenna, leaning in: "Well, look at you, starting to sound like one of those conspiracy theorists. What's next? Are you going to tell me the moon landing was faked?"

Sam, with a half-smile, counters: "No, nothing like that. But, don't you find it odd how we just accepted all these changes without question? It's like we traded our freedom for a bit of convenience and security."

Their conversation marks a turning point for Sam. The doubts and questions that were mere whispers in his mind are now finding a voice, expressing a growing unease with the status quo.

In the days that follow, Sam's interactions with his colleagues and friends begin to change. He starts noticing the small ways in which personal freedoms have been eroded, the subtle yet pervasive influence of the global governance in everyday life.

At work, while discussing the latest social credit regulations with a coworker, Tom, Sam can't help but express his skepticism: "Don't you think it's a bit much? Yesterday, I lost points for jaywalking. Jaywalking,

Tom! It's like we're children being constantly watched over by a nanny state."

Tom, always the pragmatist, shrugs: "Better safe and watched than sorry, I guess. At least, that's what they keep telling us."

These interactions, once unremarkable, now serve as catalysts, deepening Sam's understanding of the world he lives in. He starts paying closer attention to the news, the government announcements, and the propaganda that fills the city's screens and billboards.

As Sam's awareness grows, so does his sense of dissonance. He finds himself increasingly at odds with the pervasive surveillance and control, his initial acceptance giving way to a simmering discontent. This change is subtle at first, a series of small realizations and questions, but steadily, it begins to reshape his perspective, setting him on a path that diverges from the complacency that once defined him.

In this narrative arc, Sam embodies the journey of awakening, a journey that many in this dystopian world might be on. His evolution from acceptance to skepticism reflects the broader theme of questioning authority and the true cost of a controlled society. Through Sam, the story invites readers to explore these questions, to see the world through the eyes of someone who is slowly realizing that the price of unquestioned governance might be too high.

Journey into Rebellion: The Unlikely Catalyst

The quaint café, with its fusion of the old world and the new, serves as the backdrop for Sam's transition from a passive observer of this controlled world to an active participant in the undercurrents of rebellion.

One evening, as the café begins to empty, Sam finds himself in an unexpected conversation with an old man, Mr. Kearns, known for his outspoken views against the global governance.

Mr. Kearns, leaning in close with a conspiratorial glint in his eye, whispers: "You know, young man, it takes more than just seeing the chains to break them. It takes courage to act, to challenge the norms."

Sam, intrigued but cautious, replies: "But what can one person really do, Mr. Kearns? It's not like I can just stand up to a global system."

Mr. Kearns, with a knowing smile, responds: "Ah, but every great wave starts with a ripple. You'd be surprised how one voice can amplify into a chorus of dissent."

This conversation ignites something within Sam. He begins to see himself not just as a cog in the machine but as a potential agent of change. The idea is daunting but exhilarating.

The next day, at work, Sam overhears his colleagues casually discussing the latest mandatory 'Citizen Wellness Check.'

Sam, unable to keep silent, interjects: "Don't you guys find it a bit intrusive, though? This whole wellness check is just another way to keep tabs on us."

His colleague, Sarah, laughs it off: "Oh, Sam, you and your sudden rebellious streak! What's next? Are you going to start a revolution with your data analysis skills?"

Sam, with a small, determined smile, retorts: "Maybe I will, Sarah. Maybe I will."

As days pass, Sam's transformation becomes more apparent. He starts questioning the norms more openly, engaging in discussions about the intrusive policies and the loss of freedoms. His apartment, once a place for solitary refuge, now becomes a hub for hushed conversations and plans for subtle acts of resistance.

During a late-night meeting with a small group of like-minded individuals, Sam finds himself volunteering for a risky endeavor — distributing underground literature critical of the global governance.

Mia, the librarian, looks at him, surprised: "Sam, I never pegged you as the rebellious type. What changed?"

Sam, with newfound conviction, answers: "I guess I realized that staying silent is just another form of consent. It's time to make some noise, however small it may be."

Through these actions, Sam becomes an unlikely catalyst for change, his journey reflecting the awakening of many who once accepted the world as it was presented to them. His transformation from a compliant citizen into a resistor, albeit a reluctant one at first, symbolizes the potential for rebellion inherent in every individual.

This narrative arc is crucial in setting the stage for the unfolding story. It demonstrates the power of awakening and the impact one individual can have in a society that values conformity above all else. Sam's journey into rebellion is not just a personal transformation but a representation of a larger movement, a ripple that signifies the beginning of a wave.

Chapter 1: The New World

Life in 2030 - A Detailed Glimpse

Daily Routines and Society

The dawn in 2030 doesn't break with a rooster's crow or the first light peeking through curtains; it begins with the soft glow of screens and the quiet hum of a smart home coming to life. Sam, our protagonist, is roused not by an alarm clock, but by a gentle voice from his AI assistant, gently nudging him into consciousness.

AI Assistant: "Good morning, Sam. It's 6:30 AM. You have a meeting at 8. Don't forget your wellness check-up is due today."

Sam, groggy and rubbing his eyes, mumbles a response, his room illuminating with the day's schedule and the latest news flashing across his wall screen.

His morning routine is a symphony of technology - from the smart mirror that recommends the day's outfit based on the weather and his schedule, to the nutritional dispenser that prepares his breakfast based on his dietary needs and health metrics.

Sam, to his AI Assistant while eating: "Do I really have to wear the blue tie? What if I'm in a red tie mood today?"

AI Assistant, in a tone that's almost too cheerful: "The blue tie complements your meeting agenda's seriousness, Sam. And remember, your Social Credit benefits from adhering to recommended attire guidelines."

Sam chuckles to himself, a small act of rebellion against a life increasingly dictated by algorithms and recommendations.

His commute to work is seamless, a driverless car smoothly navigating the bustling city streets. Along the way, billboards flash with advertisements tailored to his recent searches and purchases, a reminder of the ever-watchful eye of consumer algorithms.

At the coffee shop, Sam places his order with a touch on the screen, his Digital ID instantly processing the payment from his CBDC account. The barista, more of an overseer for the automated coffee machines than a craftsman of caffeinated beverages, gives a polite nod.

Barista: "Your usual, Sam? The system suggests trying the new Caramel Macchiato. It's trending in your consumer profile."

Sam, with a smirk: "I'll stick with the usual, thanks. I'm not quite ready to have my coffee choices dictated by what's trending."

The exchange, light-hearted on the surface, belies Sam's growing weariness of a life where choices are often presented as suggestions but feel more like mandates.

At work, Sam's interactions are a blend of in-person and digital. Meetings are conducted with colleagues who are physically present and others who join as holograms. The workplace is a blend of efficiency and surveillance, productivity monitored, and social interactions subtly encouraged to foster a 'healthy and collaborative' environment.

Co-worker, joking during a break: "Hey Sam, careful with the water cooler talk. You wouldn't want to drop a Social Credit point for idle gossip."

Sam, playing along but with a hint of sincerity: "Right, because heaven forbid we have an unmonitored conversation."

The day-to-day life in 2030, as experienced by Sam and millions of others, is a tapestry of convenience and control, interwoven and indistinguishable. The Digital IDs and CBDCs are not just tools of transaction; they are gatekeepers of a lifestyle, arbiters of access, and markers of societal standing.

In this world, Sam's journey from a passive participant to a questioning observer marks the beginning of an awakening, a realization that the seamless integration of technology in every aspect of life is not just a marvel of progress, but a leash of compliance, subtly yet firmly guiding every choice and every step.

Impact on Personal Freedom

As the day unfolds, the undercurrents of a controlled society become increasingly apparent in the lives of its citizens, including Sam.

In the bustling lunch hour, Sam decides to purchase a sandwich from a nearby automated food kiosk. He selects his usual, but the screen flickers with a warning.

Kiosk Screen: "Selection Denied. Your recent health metrics indicate an excess of sodium. Please select a healthier option."

Sam, with a sigh of resignation, opts for a salad instead, his choice dictated more by the system's analysis of his health data than his actual preference.

Sam, muttering under his breath: "Guess my lunch is no longer just my business. Next, they'll be telling me how to chew."

Later, Sam decides to visit a tech store to browse for a new smartwatch. As he admires a high-end model, a store attendant approaches him.

Store Attendant, with a polite yet distant smile: "I'm sorry, sir, but that model is not recommended for your current Social Credit tier. Might I suggest something more... suited to your profile?"

Sam's expression shifts from interest to a subtle blend of embarrassment and frustration.

Sam, trying to brush it off with humor: "Of course, how silly of me. I wouldn't want to strain my wrist with something too fancy."

The attendant gives a courteous nod, not catching the sarcasm in Sam's tone, and guides him to a less advanced section of the store.

These instances, seemingly minor and inconsequential, paint a larger picture of the erosion of personal freedom. Choices, once taken for granted, are now filtered through a lens of algorithms and social credit evaluations. The technology, integrated into every aspect of life, subtly steers behaviors and decisions, nudging citizens along a path deemed appropriate by unseen arbiters.

As Sam returns to his routine, the weight of these realizations begins to settle in. The world around him, once a marvel of advancement, now feels more like a gilded cage – shiny and appealing from a distance, but confining upon a closer look.

In a reflective moment at the café, Sam shares his thoughts with Jenna:

Sam: "It's like we're living in a world where our choices aren't really our own. Every step, every purchase, every bite we take is scrutinized and scored. Where's the freedom in that?"

Jenna, empathetically: "It's the price we pay for convenience, I guess. But you're right, it does feel like we're trading bits of ourselves for it."

This conversation encapsulates the growing unease among the populace. The subtle yet pervasive control exerts a quiet pressure on their lives, shaping their experiences in ways they are only just beginning to comprehend. For Sam, this realization is the first step on a path that will lead him from complacency to a desire for something more – a life where freedom is not just a concept in the pages of a history book, but a tangible, everyday reality.

Cultural Shifts

In the world of 2030, the café serves as a microcosm where the impact of cultural shifts is distinctly visible. Here, amidst the aroma of coffee and the quiet hum of conversation, one can observe the new norms of social interaction and the evolving dynamics of trust.

Sam, having finished his workday, meets Jenna and a few other friends at the café. Their greetings, once warm hugs or firm handshakes, are now replaced by polite nods and brief eye contact, a byproduct of a culture where physical contact is deemed unnecessary and potentially risky.

Jenna, with a touch of irony in her voice, comments: "Remember when people used to shake hands? Now, it's like we're all carrying a plague. Virtual hugs just don't have the same feel, do they?"

Sam, with a wry smile: "I guess it's efficient, though. No more awkward 'do we hug or shake hands' moments."

Their laughter, albeit genuine, carries an undercurrent of nostalgia for a time when human interactions were not so heavily mediated by technology and fear of social missteps.

As they sit down, their conversation turns to the latest community news, displayed on the café's digital bulletin board. Personal achievements, social events, and even minor transgressions are publicly shared, contributing to an environment where privacy is a relic of the past, and one's life is an open digital book.

Mike, a friend from Sam's college days, remarks: "Did you see? Clara got docked points for hosting a party. Too many people, they said. Guess socializing is the new rebellion."

Sam, half-jokingly, responds: "Better be careful, Mike. Your Social Score can't handle much more 'rebellion'."

The conversation highlights how trust is built and eroded in this new world. Social credit scores, public profiles, and digital footprints have become the yardsticks by which people measure trustworthiness and social worth. Relationships, both personal and professional, are increasingly influenced by these digital indicators, leading to a society where genuine connections are harder to forge and maintain.

As the evening progresses, the group engages in a lively debate about a recent art exhibition, accessible only via virtual reality (VR) platforms. The exhibition, an attempt to replicate the experience of a physical gallery, has sparked discussions about the role of technology in experiencing art and culture.

Liz, an art enthusiast in the group, sighs: "It's just not the same, you know? Seeing a painting on a VR headset versus standing in front of it. We're losing touch with the real world."

Sam, contemplative, adds: "It's like we're living in a world of simulations. Real experiences are becoming rare commodities."

Their discussion reflects a broader societal trend — the gradual replacement of direct experiences with digital or simulated alternatives, further distancing people from the tangible world and each other.

In these cultural shifts, one can see the profound impact of technology on the fabric of society. The erosion of traditional forms of interaction, the public display of private lives, and the virtualization of experiences have created a world where the line between reality and simulation blurs, where human connections are strained under the weight of digital oversight, and where trust is as much a matter of data as it is of human judgment.

Through Sam and his friends' experiences, the novel paints a picture of a society navigating these shifts, struggling to hold onto the essence of human connection amidst a sea of digital waves.

Introduction to Global Landscape

Demise of Nation-States

In the dimly lit café, where remnants of the old world linger amidst the encroaching shadows of the new, the conversation among Sam and his friends takes a turn towards the broader changes sweeping their reality - the demise of traditional nation-states and the rise of a singular global governance entity.

Sam, his tone laced with a mix of incredulity and resignation, starts: "Can you believe there was a time when we had different countries? Now, it's just one big, happy Global Union."

Jenna, sipping her coffee, replies with a smirk: "Happy? That's one way to put it. More like one big, nosy family where everyone's in your business."

Laughter echoes around the table, but there's an underlying current of disquiet. This shift from diverse nation-states to a monolithic global entity has not been seamless. For many, like Sam, it's a loss of a part of their identity - a connection to a homeland with its unique culture, traditions, and history.

Mike, always the history buff, adds: "I miss the days when traveling meant experiencing a new country, not just a different zone of the Global Union. Remember passports?"

Liz, with a nostalgic sigh: "Yeah, and how every country had its own charm, its own story. Now it's like we're all characters in a bland, universal script."

The conversation reveals how this geopolitical shift has affected their sense of belonging and identity. The rich tapestry of the world, once colored by the distinct hues of individual nation-states, now seems homogenized under the banner of global governance.

As they continue to talk, the impact of this change on their personal lives becomes apparent. The demise of nation-states has not only altered the geopolitical landscape but also the very fabric of individual identity. Sam, who once took pride in his cultural heritage, now finds himself grappling with a sense of loss, a void where a part of his identity used to reside.

Sam, reflecting on his childhood memories, shares: "I remember celebrating national holidays with my family, each with its own traditions. Now, it's just 'Global Unity Day.' Feels like we traded our stories for a generic one."

Jenna, touching Sam's hand in a rare moment of physical connection, offers comfort: "Maybe, but they can't take our memories, Sam. We still have those."

Their exchange captures a central theme of the novel - the erosion of cultural diversity and the homogenization of identities in a world striving for uniform governance. It's a world where the nuances of individual and collective identities are overshadowed by a broader, more impersonal narrative.

Through Sam and his friends, the story explores the profound implications of this global shift - not just at a macro level but in the intimate alleys of personal identity and cultural belonging. The loss of nation-states is not just a political phenomenon; it's a deeply personal one, affecting how individuals connect with their past, perceive their present, and envision their future in a world that's becoming increasingly unrecognizable.

Role of Super-Corporations

As the evening in the café wears on, the discussion among Sam and his friends shifts to a topic that's become a staple in conversations around the world: the omnipresent role of super-corporations in their daily lives.

Sam, his voice tinged with a blend of awe and cynicism, broaches the topic: "You know, it's like the whole world is just a playground for these super-corporations. They're more powerful than countries used to be."

Jenna, with her characteristic sharp wit, quips: "Oh, absolutely. I mean, who needs a government when you've got CorpLife managing your health, your finances, and even your dating life?"

Laughter erupts at the table, but it's evident that the humor is a thin veil over a growing unease. These super-corporations, entities that have grown to wield unprecedented influence, have become an inescapable part of their existence. They control everything from the news people receive to the products they consume, blurring the lines between corporate power and personal choice.

Mike, leaning in, adds conspiratorially: "Did you hear about the latest? CorpLife's new 'Happiness Initiative.' They say they can predict and manage your life choices for maximum happiness. As if a corporation knows what makes us happy."

Liz, rolling her eyes: "Next thing you know, they'll be choosing our pets for us. 'Our algorithm suggests a goldfish is the ideal pet for you.'"

Their banter reflects a deep-seated concern about the overreach of these corporations. Gone are the days when companies simply sold products or services. Now, they dictate lifestyles, control access to resources, and even influence personal decisions under the guise of efficiency and optimization.

Sam, who works as a data analyst for one of these super-corporations, feels this more acutely than most. Every day, he sees firsthand how data is used to shape consumer behavior and personal choices.

Sam, with a hint of resignation: "It's scary how much they know about us. Sometimes, I feel like I'm just a set of data points to be analyzed and monetized."

Jenna, sympathetically: "That's because, to them, you are, Sam. We all are. But hey, at least the data says we're a bunch of happy consumers, right?"

As the group delves deeper into the discussion, it becomes clear that these super-corporations are more than just powerful entities in the economy. They've become embedded in the social fabric, influencing not just what people buy or how they live, but also how they think and interact with each other.

Through this conversation, the novel sheds light on the pervasive influence of super-corporations in the world of 2030. They're not just a backdrop to the story but are central to understanding the societal dynamics at play. Their role in shaping every aspect of life represents a new form of power, one that transcends traditional boundaries and poses new challenges to personal autonomy and freedom.

In this setting, Sam and his friends represent the everyday people who navigate this corporatized world, each grappling with the implications of living under the shadow of entities whose motives and methods are as influential as they are opaque.

Media and Propaganda

The cozy confines of the café, with its mix of old-world charm and modern patrons, serve as an ideal setting for Sam and his friends to discuss another pervasive aspect of their lives in 2030 – the role of media and propaganda in shaping public perception.

Sam, glancing at the large digital news display on the café wall, remarks cynically: "Have you noticed how the news always seems to paint the Global Union in such radiant colors? It's like watching a never-ending parade of their greatness."

Jenna, sipping her coffee, adds: "Oh, absolutely. It's all 'unity this' and 'progress that'. Makes you wonder what they're not telling us in between the lines of all this grandeur."

The group shares a knowing look, aware of the stark contrast between the media's glossy portrayal of the world and the reality of their everyday experiences.

Mike, a bit more pointedly, says: "It's not just the news. Have you seen the latest 'Citizen's Duty' ads? They make conforming to the Social Credit System look like the highest form of patriotism."

Liz, with a laugh: "Yeah, because nothing says freedom like being rewarded for following orders. They should just give us all medals for being good little citizens."

Their banter, though light-hearted, underscores a deeper unease about the omnipresent nature of media propaganda. The news channels, social media platforms, and even advertising have become tools for the global regime to disseminate its narrative, a narrative that carefully glosses over any flaws or failures.

Sam, reflecting on his work in data analysis, contributes a more somber note to the conversation.

Sam, pensively: "It's all about data and perception management. We analyze public reactions, tweak the message, and feed it back through the channels. It's like a loop, but each time, the truth gets more and more diluted."

The realization that their opinions, beliefs, and even emotions are being manipulated and shaped by a carefully orchestrated media strategy is a bitter pill to swallow.

Jenna, with a hint of defiance: "So, what do we do? Just accept it as the new normal?"

Sam, with a newfound determination in his voice: "No, we question it, Jenna. We read between the lines, and we look for the truth, even if it's hidden in a mountain of propaganda."

This exchange encapsulates the critical role media and propaganda play in the world of 2030. The global regime, with its control over the media, manufactures a narrative that promotes unity and progress, while quietly suppressing dissent and painting a sanitized picture of reality.

Through the eyes of Sam and his friends, the novel explores the impact of this relentless propaganda on the human psyche — how it shapes perceptions, molds opinions, and, in some cases, awakens a desire to seek out the obscured truth. It's a world where the media is not just a source of information but a tool of governance, guiding public opinion with a mix of glossy imagery and subtle manipulation.

Protagonist's Perspective and Inner Conflict

Initial Acceptance

In the dim, ambient lighting of the café, Sam's initial acceptance of the new world order becomes a topic of introspection and gentle ribbing among his friends.

Jenna, with a teasing tone: "Remember when Sam here was all gung-ho about the Global Union? 'It's for the greater good,' he said. 'Efficiency and unity,' he said."

Sam, with a sheepish grin, admits: "Yeah, I bought into the whole spiel. Unified currency, global healthcare, streamlined governance - it all sounded so... neat."

The group chuckles, but there's an understanding in their laughter. They, too, had once believed in the promise of a better world, seduced by the allure of a system that promised to erase the chaos and disparities of the old nation-states.

Mike, leaning back in his chair, adds: "We all did, to some extent. It was like a shiny new toy – all sleek and full of promise. But then, we started to notice the strings attached."

Sam's journey from acceptance to skepticism is not unique; it mirrors a broader societal trend. Initially, the unification under a global regime seemed to be the answer to many of the world's problems - a way to bridge divides and create a more equitable and efficient society.

Liz, with a hint of sarcasm: "Equitable, sure, as long as you don't mind having your choices made for you. What's a little freedom compared to world peace, right?"

The conversation takes a more serious turn as Sam reflects on his journey.

Sam, thoughtfully: "It's strange how the lines blur. At first, the control was subtle - for our safety, for our health. But then, it started to encroach on everything... our choices, our privacy."

This introspection marks the beginning of Sam's inner conflict. The realization that the initial benefits of the global system came at the cost of personal freedoms and autonomy starts to weigh heavily on him. The narrative begins to explore the complexity of Sam's character - a man who, like many, wanted to believe in a utopian vision but now grapples with the reality of its implementation.

Jenna, placing a comforting hand on Sam's shoulder: "It's not your fault, Sam. We all wanted to believe in a better world. It's just that... well, we didn't read the fine print."

Sam's initial acceptance of the new order, influenced by a combination of propaganda and genuine hope for a unified global system, sets the stage for his journey. As he begins to confront the darker aspects of this new world, his internal struggle reflects the broader question facing society: At what point does the price for unity and efficiency become too high? Sam's character development, starting from this point of acceptance, promises to take the reader on a journey of awakening and resistance, as he navigates the complexities of a world where the line between utopia and dystopia is increasingly blurred.

Hints of Discontent

In the heart of the bustling café, under the soft glow of ambient lights, Sam's growing discontent becomes increasingly evident, surfacing in his interactions and observations.

The conversation takes a turn as Sam recounts a recent incident at work.

Sam, with a furrowed brow, shares: "I was analyzing user data yesterday, and I couldn't shake off this feeling... It's like we're just cogs in a giant machine, our data fueling its insatiable appetite."

Jenna, looking concerned, probes further: "But you've always been passionate about data, Sam. What's changed?"

Sam, pausing to find the right words: "I guess... it's the realization that we're not just analyzing data. We're analyzing lives. There's something unsettling about that."

Sam's revelation is a small yet significant moment, highlighting his inner turmoil. It's a shift from seeing his role as just a job to recognizing the broader implications of his work on society.

Later, while walking through the city, Sam's discomfort becomes more palpable. The towering digital billboards, once marvels of technology, now seem to loom over him, their ever-present messages dictating what to buy, how to live, and what to believe.

Sam, gazing up at a billboard promoting the latest Global Union initiative, mutters under his breath: "'Unity in conformity,' more like. Where's the space for individual thought?"

This inner monologue is interrupted as Sam overhears a conversation between two passersby, discussing the recent mandatory installation of home surveillance devices for 'citizen safety.'

Passerby 1, with a hint of pride: "I've got mine installed yesterday. It's for our security, you know. Can't be too safe these days."

Passerby 2, somewhat apprehensively: "Yeah, but doesn't it bother you? Having your home watched all the time?"

Passerby 1, dismissively: "If you've got nothing to hide, you've got nothing to fear, right?"

This overheard conversation further fuels Sam's growing unease. The adage, 'nothing to hide, nothing to fear,' once a comforting reassurance, now rings hollow in his ears.

As the day ends and Sam finds himself alone in his apartment, his sense of disquiet deepens. The smart devices around him, once symbols of convenience and connectivity, now feel like silent sentinels, watching his every move.

Sam, speaking to the quiet of his room: "Is this it, then? Living in a world where privacy is a luxury and every step is monitored and measured?"

These moments of introspection and observation mark the beginning of a significant shift in Sam's perspective. The novel begins to weave a narrative of subtle yet growing discontent, as Sam starts to question the world he lives in. This internal conflict is not just a personal struggle; it mirrors the collective unease of a society grappling with the implications of a life under constant scrutiny. Through Sam, the story explores the themes of individuality, freedom, and the cost of security in a world where the line between protection and control is increasingly blurred.

Foreshadowing of Change

As the evening draws to a close in the café, a chance encounter serves as the catalyst for a profound shift in Sam's journey. The walls, adorned with remnants of a bygone era, bear witness to the foreshadowing of change.

The catalyst arrives in the form of an old college friend, Derek, who Sam bumps into as he's leaving. Derek, known for his activist leanings, greets him enthusiastically: "Sam! It's been ages. You look... well, you look like you've seen a ghost."

Sam, surprised and somewhat relieved to see a familiar face from his past, responds: "Hey, Derek. Just the usual ghosts of a world that's moving too fast for its own good."

As they step outside the café, Derek's demeanor shifts to something more serious. He glances around cautiously before speaking.

Derek, in a hushed tone: "Sam, I know we lost touch, but I've heard about your work with data analysis. I need your help. There's something big happening, something that could expose the Global Union for what it really is."

Sam's eyes widen, a mix of intrigue and apprehension flickering across his face.

Sam, with a hint of skepticism: "Derek, what are you talking about? Expose the Global Union? That's... that's huge."

Derek, with a sense of urgency: "I can't say much here. It's not safe. But meet me tomorrow at the old library. There's something I need to show you. It could change everything."

The conversation is brief, but the impact is immediate and profound. As Derek disappears into the night, Sam stands there, a myriad of emotions swirling within him.

The chapter closes with Sam alone in his apartment, staring out the window at the cityscape bathed in the glow of neon lights. His mind races with thoughts of Derek's words, the potential dangers of getting involved, and the possibility of uncovering a truth that could shake the very foundations of the world he knows.

Sam, speaking to himself in the quiet of his room: "What have I gotten myself into? This could be the chance to make a difference, to do something meaningful... or it could be the biggest mistake of my life."

This moment of foreshadowing sets the stage for Sam's transformative journey ahead. It hints at the internal conflicts he will face and the choices he will have to make as he moves from a passive observer to an active participant in a world ripe for change. The revelation from Derek serves as the spark that ignites the dormant fire within Sam, propelling him towards a path of resistance and discovery.

The chapter ends on a note of anticipation and uncertainty, leaving the reader eager to follow Sam on his journey into the unknown, where the lines between right and wrong, truth and propaganda, are blurred, and the stakes are higher than ever.

Chapter 2: Awakening to Reality

Initial Revelations

A Day of Unrest

The chapter begins with Sam, our protagonist, stepping into a day that would mark the beginning of his awakening to the stark realities of his world in 2030.

As Sam commutes to work, the city feels different. The usual hum of activity is replaced by an undercurrent of tension. On the streets, digital billboards flash with the latest Global Union propaganda, but today, they are juxtaposed against a group of silent protestors, their mouths covered with tape, holding signs that read, "Freedom of Speech is not Algorithm Approved."

Sam, observing the scene, mutters to himself: "Didn't think I'd see a real protest in this age. Guess not everyone's sold on the Global Union's grand plan."

Arriving at work, Sam finds his colleagues huddled around a screen, watching a news report about the protest. The report labels the protestors as 'disruptors of peace,' accusing them of spreading misinformation.

Colleague 1, shaking her head: "Can you believe these people? Disturbing the peace over some conspiracy theories."

Colleague 2, with a smirk: "Yeah, because the Global Union is so oppressive. I mean, they only monitor our every move and thought for our own good, right?"

The sarcasm isn't lost on Sam. It's a stark reminder of how deeply ingrained the Global Union's narrative has become in the psyche of its citizens.

During lunch, Sam decides to walk past the protest site. The protestors are gone, but the air is still heavy with their presence. A digital flyer on his phone buzzes with a notification, warning citizens to avoid 'unauthorized gatherings' for their safety.

Sam, speaking under his breath: "'Unauthorized gatherings.' Is that what we're calling free assembly these days?"

The day takes another turn when Sam overhears a conversation between two strangers in a café.

Stranger 1: "You heard about the new surveillance upgrade, right? They say it's going to predict our needs before we even know them."

Stranger 2, laughing: "Great, just what I need. A system that tells me I need a diet before I even order a donut."

Sam chuckles, but the humor is tinged with unease. The line between convenience and control is blurring rapidly.

Returning home, Sam's usual routine feels hollow. The news, the screens, the endless stream of notifications – they all seem to echo a narrative that he's starting to question. The day's events, contrasting sharply with his routine life, have sown seeds of doubt and unrest in his mind.

Sam, staring at his reflection in the mirror: "What if there's more to the story than what we're being fed? What if we're all just characters in a script written by the Global Union?"

This day of unrest marks the beginning of Sam's journey towards a deeper understanding of his world. The acts of rebellion, the encounters with propaganda, and the whispers of dissent have started to chip away at his acceptance of the world as he knows it. The chapter ends with Sam poised on the brink of a personal revolution, his eyes opening to the realities that lie beneath the surface of the Global Union's polished façade.

Whispers of Dissent

The day's unusual events lead Sam to a small, almost forgotten part of the city where whispers of dissent still breathe in hushed tones. He finds himself in an old bookstore, its shelves laden with books from a bygone era, a stark contrast to the digital archives that have become the norm.

Bookstore Owner, noticing Sam's curious gaze at a section of prohibited books, remarks quietly: "You won't find these in your digital library. Too much truth for the Global Union's liking."

Sam, intrigued by the owner's boldness, browses through the books, his fingers tracing the spines of history and philosophy texts that are no longer part of the approved curriculum.

Sam, half-jokingly: "What, no self-help books on how to improve your Social Credit Score?"

Bookstore Owner, with a wry smile: "Afraid not. My selection tends to lean more towards 'how to think' than 'what to think.'"

This encounter marks Sam's first real introduction to the underground networks that operate on the fringes of society. The bookstore owner, sensing Sam's growing curiosity, subtly directs him to a back room where a small group is gathered, engaged in a spirited discussion.

Sam overhears snippets of conversation that challenge the official narratives. Topics range from suppressed scientific studies to censored historical events, painting a picture of a world much more complex and less benevolent than the one portrayed by the Global Union.

A woman in the group, speaking passionately: "They control the information, and in doing so, they control us. But the truth has a way of coming out, no matter how hard they try to suppress it."

Sam feels a mixture of excitement and apprehension. This is the first time he's encountered open dissent, and the raw honesty of the conversation both scares and invigorates him.

Sam, cautiously joining the conversation: "Isn't it dangerous, talking like this? What if you're caught?"

A man across the table, with a spark of defiance in his eyes, responds: "Dangerous? Maybe. Necessary? Absolutely. Silence is what they want from us, but silence is complicity."

As the meeting concludes, Sam leaves the bookstore with a mind swirling with new ideas and questions. The whispers of dissent have opened a door he never knew existed, offering a glimpse into a world where not everyone is content to follow the script written by those in power.

Sam, speaking to himself as he walks through the quiet streets: "What else don't I know? What other lies have we been fed?"

This night marks a significant turning point for Sam. The once unquestioning citizen is now a man teetering on the edge of a new reality, one where dissent and truth-seeking are the keys to understanding the true nature of the world he lives in. The chapter ends with Sam's resolve to explore these underground networks further, setting him on a path that could lead to either enlightenment or danger.

Personal Connection

The revelations at the underground bookstore linger in Sam's mind as he makes his way to an old, familiar part of town. Here, he plans to meet his sister, Lucy, who has always had a rebellious streak, much to the chagrin of their more conformist parents.

Lucy, greeting Sam with a sly grin: "Welcome to the dark side, brother. Never thought I'd see you in this part of town voluntarily."

Sam, with a hint of defensiveness: "It's not like I'm here to join a secret rebellion, Lucy. Just wanted to catch up."

They find a quiet corner in a small, rundown café – a stark contrast to the polished, high-tech establishments that now dominate the city. As they talk, Lucy shares her experiences working at a community clinic in the underprivileged sector, where the glossy veneer of the Global Union's propaganda fades to reveal a harsher reality.

Lucy, her voice a mix of frustration and passion: "You should see it, Sam. People are struggling. The 'unified healthcare system' isn't as equal as they make it out to be. It's all about your Social Credit here too."

Sam listens, his sister's words adding a new layer of complexity to his understanding of the world. The personal connection to Lucy's experiences in the clinic makes the issues more tangible, more emotionally charged.

Sam, troubled: "But the news always talks about healthcare advancements, about how everyone's covered."

Lucy, snorting in disbelief: "Yeah, and I bet they also tell you we all sing 'Kumbaya' at the end of each day. Sam, wake up. There's a whole world out there that's nothing like what they show you."

As they continue their conversation, Lucy reveals her involvement in grassroots movements aimed at bringing attention to these disparities.

Lucy, leaning in closer: "I've been working with a group of doctors and activists. We're trying to set up an independent network to help those who fall through the cracks."

Sam, intrigued and concerned: "Isn't that risky? What if you get caught?"

Lucy, with a determined glint in her eye: "It's riskier to do nothing, Sam. Sometimes, you have to stand up for what's right, even if it means standing against the tide."

This meeting with Lucy serves as a turning point for Sam. Her involvement in the resistance movement and her firsthand accounts of the system's failings provide a personal anchor to the dissenting views he's recently encountered. It's no longer just about abstract concepts or hidden truths; it's about his sister, her struggles, and her fight for a cause she believes in.

As Sam leaves the café, his sister's parting words resonate with him.

Lucy, with a half-joking, half-serious tone: "Think about it, Sam. Maybe there's a rebel in you yet."

The chapter closes with Sam walking through the city streets, deep in thought. Lucy's words and the day's experiences have stirred something within him. A once complacent citizen is now on the cusp of a journey that could change not just his life but also the very fabric of the society he thought he knew. The personal connection to the resistance, through Lucy, has set Sam on a path that is fraught with danger, but also filled with the potential for profound change.

Encounter with the Resistance

Unexpected Meeting

The following day, still reeling from the conversations with his sister and the revelations at the bookstore, Sam's routine takes an unexpected turn. Walking through a less frequented part of the city, he notices a commotion in an alleyway. Curiosity piqued, he cautiously approaches.

In the alley, he finds a small group of people huddled around a young woman, who appears to be injured. The air is thick with tension, and the group's anxious glances reveal their fear of being discovered.

Sam, with a mix of concern and confusion: "Hey, is everything okay here? Does she need a doctor?"

One of the group members, a man with a wary look, responds tersely: "She's fine. Just tripped, that's all. No need for doctors."

Sam, not convinced but sensing the group's apprehension, offers his assistance.

Sam, trying to sound nonchalant: "I'm no doctor, but I know a thing or two about first aid. Let me help."

Reluctantly, the group allows Sam to approach. As he tends to the woman's injury, he overhears snippets of their conversation – words like "meeting" and "safe house" catch his attention.

Injured Woman, whispering to Sam as he bandages her ankle: "Thank you. We're... we're not what they say we are. We're just trying to make things right."

Sam, intrigued, whispers back: "Who are 'they'? What are you trying to do?"

Before she can answer, a distant siren wails, and the group quickly disperses, leaving Sam and the woman alone in the alley.

Sam, helping her to her feet: "You're part of the resistance, aren't you? The real one, not the one they show on the news."

The Woman, with a hint of a smile, despite the pain: "And you're full of surprises, Sam. Most people wouldn't have stopped to help."

She hands him a small, crumpled piece of paper with an address and a time scribbled on it.

The Woman, as she limps away: "If you want to know more, come to this address tonight. But be careful, they're always watching."

Sam stands there for a moment, the paper in his hand, a gateway to a world he's only just beginning to understand. This unexpected meeting, a chance encounter, has suddenly thrust him closer to the heart of the resistance.

The chapter ends with Sam returning to the routine of his day, but his mind is far from the spreadsheets and data analysis in front of him. The encounter in the alley has awakened a curiosity, a desire to understand the truth behind the façade of the world he lives in. The prospect of attending the meeting is both daunting and exhilarating – a step into the unknown that could alter the course of his life forever.

Diverse Resistance Group

Later that evening, Sam finds himself standing before an unassuming building, the address from the crumpled paper in his hand. He takes a deep breath and steps inside, entering a dimly lit room where a small group of people are gathered. Each face tells a story of dissent, of a life that deviated from the prescribed path of the Global Union.

As Sam is introduced to the group, he learns of their diverse backgrounds, each contributing to a tapestry of resistance against the prevailing regime.

First, there's Leo, a former corporate executive: "I used to help design the algorithms that predict consumer behavior. I knew something was off when they started asking for data points on political leanings. That's when I got out."

Sam, impressed and somewhat intimidated, replies: "That's... quite a leap from corporate life to this."

Leo, with a wry grin: "Let's just say, I prefer using my powers for good now."

Next, he meets Maya, a disillusioned government worker, who shares her story with a mix of anger and determination.

Maya: "I saw things, data manipulations, silencing of voices... I couldn't be part of it anymore. We're supposed to serve the people, not control them."

Sam, increasingly intrigued, responds: "And now you're here, fighting against the very system you were part of."

Maya, nodding: "It's the only way to make things right."

In the corner of the room, a young woman, Ava, sketches fervently in her notebook. Her vibrant, rebellious art adorns the walls of the hideout.

Ava, without looking up: "Art is truth. They can't silence that. Each piece I create is a strike against their sterile world."

Sam, examining her artwork: "It's incredible. You're really putting yourself out there with these."

Ava, with a hint of defiance: "What's the point of art if it doesn't say something, if it doesn't risk something?"

The group, though small, represents a cross-section of society - individuals who, for various reasons, have found themselves at odds with the system. Their stories and backgrounds provide a rich backdrop to the resistance, illustrating that dissent comes from all walks of life.

As the meeting progresses, Sam listens intently, his initial apprehension giving way to a growing sense of camaraderie. He realizes that the resistance is not just a faceless entity but a collection of individuals, each with their own story of awakening and defiance.

Sam, as the meeting concludes: "I never knew there were so many layers to what's happening. It's like I've been asleep this whole time."

Leo, clapping him on the back: "Welcome to the waking world, Sam. It's a bit messier, but it's real."

This encounter marks a significant development in Sam's character. He's no longer just an observer; he's become part of something larger - a d verse group united in their quest for truth and freedom. The chapter ends with Sam feeling a newfound sense of purpose, a connection to a cause that transcends his individual doubts and fears.

First Impressions

As Sam takes in the scene of the resistance meeting, his emotions are a whirlwind of skepticism, fear, and burgeoning curiosity. The air in the room is thick with a sense of urgency and determination that Sam finds both intimidating and exhilarating.

Sam, voicing his apprehension: "This is all... a lot to take in. I mean, aren't you afraid of what could happen if you're caught?"

Leo, with a knowing smile: "Fear is a luxury we can't afford, Sam. Besides, living in blind compliance is its own kind of prison."

Sam's eyes dart around the room, taking in each member of the group. He feels out of place, like a bystander who has stumbled onto a stage where a play is already in progress.

Maya, sensing his discomfort, reassures him: "We've all been where you are, Sam. It's okay to be skeptical. That's how we know you're thinking for yourself."

Sam, half-jokingly: "Well, I'm great at skepticism. It's the potential rebellion I'm not so sure about."

His attempt at humor masks a deeper conflict within. On one hand, Sam is drawn to the raw honesty and passion of the group. On the other, he's acutely aware of the risks involved in aligning with them.

Ava, looking up from her sketches, adds playfully: "Think of it as an adventure, Sam. The kind where you might just help save the world."

Sam, with a wry laugh: "No pressure, right? Just a casual world-saving adventure."

Despite his efforts to lighten the mood, Sam can't shake off the gravity of the situation. The stories and experiences shared by the group members are starkly different from the world he's known — a world where compliance is rewarded, and dissent is a dangerous path.

As the meeting progresses, Sam's initial skepticism gives way to a growing intrigue. The stories he hears and the people he meets are opening his eyes to realities he had never considered. The resistance is not just a shadowy organization but a collection of real people with genuine concerns and hopes for a different future.

The chapter ends with Sam leaving the meeting deep in thought. His curiosity has been piqued, but so has his sense of caution. The decision to get involved or remain a passive observer looms large, a decision that could alter the course of his life.

Sam, to himself as he walks home: "What am I getting myself into? Can I really be part of something like this?"

Sam's internal conflict and apprehension set the stage for his character development. His journey from skepticism to active involvement will be fraught with challenges and self-doubt, but also with growth and discovery. The chapter closes on this note of uncertainty, reflecting the internal struggle that many face when confronted with the choice to either challenge the status quo or remain safely within its confines.

The World Through New Eyes

Altered Perceptions

In the days following the resistance meeting, Sam finds himself viewing the world through a new lens. The streets he walks, the workplace he frequents, even the café he loves, all seem different now, tainted by his newfound knowledge of the reality lurking beneath the surface.

Sam, sharing his thoughts with Jenna at their usual café meetup: "You ever notice how those 'security' cameras are positioned? It's like they're more interested in watching us than keeping us safe."

Jenna, with a hint of sarcasm: "What, you mean you don't feel cuddled in the warm embrace of Big Brother's ever-watchful eyes?"

Sam chuckles, but the laughter doesn't quite reach his eyes. His gaze drifts to a nearby camera, its unblinking lens a constant reminder of the surveillance state they live in.

Walking to work, Sam's attention is caught by the massive digital bil boards that line the city streets, their messages of unity and progress now appearing hollow and propagandistic.

Sam, muttering to himself: "Unity, sure, as long as you toe the line. 'Progress' – but at what cost?"

At work, the daily data analysis that once seemed routine now feels intrusive. Sam begins to question the ethics behind the information he's processing. Each piece of data represents a person, a life being quantified and categorized.

Sam, during a lunch break conversation with a colleague: "Do you ever think about the data we handle? We're not just crunching numbers; we're delving into people's private lives."

Colleague, nonchalantly: "It's just data, Sam. Don't overthink it. It's not like we're the ones using it to control people."

Sam's response is a forced smile, but internally, he feels a growing sense of disquiet. The casual dismissal of privacy by those around him underscores the normalization of surveillance in their society.

As he walks home that evening, Sam notices things he previously ignored – the facial recognition scanners at every corner, the drones buzzing overhead, the constant presence of screens broadcasting government-approved messages. The city, once a vibrant hub of life and activity, now feels like a carefully staged play, with each citizen unknowingly playing their assigned role.

Sam, in a reflective moment at home: "I used to think all this was for our benefit, for safety and efficiency. But now, it feels like we're all just pieces in a larger game, a game where we don't even know the rules."

This change in perception marks a significant turning point in Sam's character arc. The once complacent data analyst is now a man burdened with the knowledge of the extent of control exerted over society. This internal struggle between his old world view and his new understanding of the pervasive surveillance and manipulation forms the crux of his journey towards awakening. The chapter ends with Sam at a crossroads, his eyes opened to the realities of his world, yet unsure of his role in challenging the status quo.

Growing Awareness

Sam's journey of awakening accelerates as he begins to notice the stark disparities between the polished propaganda of the Global Union and the grim realities of its governance.

One morning, on his way to work, Sam witnesses an unsettling scene. A man, his face etched with despair, is being escorted out of a building by security. His access has been revoked, a clear indication of a low Social Credit Score.

Bystander, whispering to Sam: "Heard he spoke out against the Union's policies. That's a quick way to tank your score."

Sam, shocked: "Just for speaking his mind?"

Bystander, with a shrug: "Freedom of speech is a high-priced commodity these days."

This incident is a stark revelation for Sam, showcasing the harsh consequences of dissent in this new world. The idea of 'freedom of speech' now seems more like a relic from a bygone era, a luxury few can afford.

The disparities become even more evident when Sam visits a different part of the city. Here, the gleaming façades give way to neglected neighborhoods, where the promises of the Global Union feel like distant echoes.

Walking through these streets, Sam sees firsthand the impact of the regime's policies on everyday people. Long lines for basic necessities, weary faces, and a palpable sense of resignation paint a picture far removed from the unity and prosperity touted by the state media.

Local Resident, noticing Sam's bewildered look: "First time on this side of the city, huh? Welcome to the real world, where the 'Global Union' is just a fancy term for 'survival of the fittest.'"

Sam, disheartened: "I had no idea it was like this."

Later, at a café, Sam overhears a conversation between two young professionals discussing the latest Union mandate.

Professional 1, in a hushed tone: "Did you hear about the new surveillance upgrade in the offices? They say it's to boost productivity, but we all know it's to keep a tighter leash on us."

Professional 2, cynically: "Productivity, right. Because what's a day at work without a healthy dose of paranoia?"

The conversation further opens Sam's eyes to the pervasive nature of the regime's control, extending even into the supposed sanctity of the workplace.

As Sam returns home that evening, his mind races with the day's revelations. The disparity between the Union's glossy exterior and the grim reality of its governance has become undeniable.

Sam, reflecting on his day: "It's like there are two worlds — the one they show us and the one they hide from us. And I've been living in the dark all this time."

This growing awareness marks a significant evolution in Sam's character. No longer just a passive observer, he is now a man grappling with the realities of a regime that is as oppressive as it is efficient. His journey of awakening is not just about seeing the world as it is but about understanding his place in it and the role he might play in challenging the status quo. The chapter ends with Sam's resolve to delve deeper into the resistance, driven by a desire to uncover the full extent of the regime's darkness and bring its truths to light.

End with a Decision

The events of the day leave Sam in a state of deep contemplation. He sits alone in his apartment that evening, the city lights casting shadows that seem to mirror the darkness of his thoughts. The disparate pieces of the world he has witnessed and learned about are coalescing into a picture that is increasingly difficult for him to ignore.

Sam, speaking aloud to himself in the solitude of his room: "It's like I've been walking with my eyes half-closed. But now, what do I do with this... this awareness?"

The silence of the room offers no answers, but the turmoil within him is reaching a crescendo. He reflects on the fear and resignation he saw in the eyes of the man with the low Social Credit Score, the desperation in the neglected neighborhoods, and the stifling control masquerading as productivity in the workplace.

Sam, wrestling with his thoughts: "I can't just sit back and pretend everything's fine, can I? But what can I, just one person, really do against something so vast, so entrenched?"

The memories of his encounters with the resistance come flooding back – the determination in Leo's eyes, Maya's passionate resolve, and Ava's defiant creativity. They represent a path that is fraught with risks but also the potential for change.

Sam, with a newfound determination: "I need to know more. I need to understand what's really going on. Maybe... maybe I can make a difference."

With this decision, the chapter comes to a close. Sam, who began as a passive citizen, comfortably ensconced in the routine of his life, has now taken the first step towards active resistance. This decision marks a pivotal moment in his journey, a transition from observer to participant, driven by a desire to seek the truth and a growing sense of responsibility to act.

Sam, as he turns off the lights and looks out at the city one last time before bed: "Tomorrow is a new day, and I'm no longer the same person I was. Let's see where this path takes me."

The chapter ends with Sam poised on the brink of a new reality, his role in the world no longer defined by the regime's dictates but by his own growing conviction to uncover and confront the truth. His decision to engage with the resistance and seek deeper understanding sets the stage for the challenges and revelations that lie ahead, promising a journey not just of external conflict but of profound personal transformation.

Chapter 3: The Seeds of Rebellion

Deepening Involvement with the Resistance

Integration into the Group

As Chapter 3 unfolds, Sam's journey takes a significant leap forward. He finds himself increasingly involved with the resistance group, his role evolving from a curious observer to an active participant.

The chapter opens with Sam attending another clandestine meeting in an abandoned warehouse on the outskirts of the city. The atmosphere is charged with a mix of determination and caution.

Leo, addressing the group: "We have a new member among us. Sam has shown a genuine interest in our cause. Let's give him a chance to prove his commitment."

Sam feels a surge of nervous excitement. He is eager to contribute but also aware of the risks involved.

Ava, with a mischievous smirk, hands Sam a stack of flyers: "Here's your first mission, should you choose to accept it – help us spread the word. But remember, stealth is key. We don't need you getting caught on your first day."

Sam, accepting the flyers with a mix of seriousness and humor: "Understood. I'll be like a shadow... a very clueless, untrained shadow."

His first task is to distribute informational flyers at various discreet locations throughout the city. The flyers contain veiled messages criticizing the regime's policies and promoting free thought. It's a seemingly small act, but one that carries significant weight in a society where such dissent is forbidden.

As he distributes the flyers, Sam feels a thrill of rebellion mixed with a sense of purpose. He's contributing to a cause he believes in, however minor his role might be at this stage.

Sam, whispering to himself as he discreetly places a flyer under a café table: "Here goes nothing. Or maybe everything."

In the following days, Sam takes on more responsibilities. He assists in organizing secret meetings, participates in discussions on strategy, and even helps with the group's efforts to hack into state-controlled media channels.

Maya, during one of the meetings, notes: "Sam's got a knack for this. His insights from his data analysis job are proving quite useful."

Sam, with a self-deprecating chuckle: "Who knew my boring day job would come in handy for clandestine activities?"

His growing involvement with the group is not without its challenges. The constant fear of being watched or caught looms over him, and the gravity of what they are doing becomes increasingly real.

Leo, in a rare moment of vulnerability, confesses to Sam: "Every step we take is a risk, Sam. But it's a risk worth taking. We're fighting for something bigger than ourselves."

This integration into the group marks a significant transformation in Sam's character. From a bystander in his own life, he becomes an active agent of change, his actions driven by a growing conviction in the righteousness of their cause.

The chapter ends with Sam feeling a deep sense of camaraderie with the group. He's no longer just Sam, the data analyst; he's Sam, the resistor, a part of something that challenges the very fabric of the society he once accepted without question.

Sam, as he looks around at the faces of his fellow resistors: "I never thought I'd find myself here, but now, I can't imagine being anywhere else. This is where I belong."

His journey into the heart of the resistance sets the stage for the challenges and adventures that lie ahead, as he navigates the dangerous waters of rebellion against a regime that tolerates no dissent.

Learning the Ropes

As Sam's involvement with the resistance deepens, he finds himself on a steep learning curve, absorbing the nuances of their operations and methods. The group operates with precision and caution, traits that Sam quickly realizes are crucial for their survival.

In a dimly lit room, hidden from the prying eyes of the surveillance state, Sam is introduced to the art of covert communication.

Maya, demonstrating a series of seemingly innocuous hand signals, explains: "We can't risk being overheard or intercepted. These signals might seem like a game, but they can save lives."

Sam, attempting to mimic the gestures, jokes: "So, if I do this, it means I need a bathroom break, not that we're about to be raided?"

Maya, with a smirk: "Exactly, though I'd avoid using that one in public unless you actually need to go."

Sam learns about encrypted messaging, the use of coded language, and the importance of always having an exit strategy. The group operates under a constant threat, and every action, every word, carries weight.

In another session, Leo introduces Sam to the intricacies of their information network – a complex web of contacts, safe houses, and secret channels for disseminating their message.

Leo, pointing to a map dotted with various markers: "Each point here represents a node in our network. We have to be careful; one wrong move could compromise the whole operation."

Sam, absorbing the complexity of it all: "It's like a giant game of chess, except the pieces are real people with real lives at stake."

As he becomes more adept at these clandestine methods, Sam also learns the importance of blending in, of maintaining the façade of a compliant citizen while working against the regime in the shadows.

Ava, as they walk through a crowded market: "Remember, the best way to hide is in plain sight. We're just ordinary people going about our day."

Sam, with a hint of irony: "Right, just a regular day of subverting the dystopian regime. Nothing out of the ordinary."

The resistance's methods are a far cry from Sam's previous life of data analysis and routine. Each day brings new challenges and skills to master, from coding secret messages to scouting locations for their meetings.

The chapter concludes with Sam successfully coordinating a small but significant operation – the distribution of underground literature in a heavily surveilled public area. It's a testament to his growing competence and the trust the group has placed in him.

Sam, whispering to Maya as they watch the operation unfold from a distance: "I never thought I'd be part of something like this. It's terrifying, but... I feel more alive than I ever have."

Sam's journey of learning the ropes of the resistance is more than just acquiring skills; it's a transformation of his very being. He's no longer the man who once accepted the world as it was presented to him; he's becoming a key player in the fight to reveal its hidden truths. The chapter ends with Sam not only more knowledgeable but more committed – a crucial step forward in his journey of rebellion.

Personal Bonds

As Sam becomes more entrenched in the resistance, he begins to forge personal bonds with its members, adding depth and complexity to his involvement. These relationships bring a human dimension to the struggle, framing the resistance not just as a political movement but as a group of individuals united by a common cause.

In a quiet corner of their makeshift headquarters, Sam finds himself frequently in conversation with Leo, whose corporate past and pragmatic approach to the resistance's activities provide a wealth of knowledge and insight.

Leo, sharing his experiences: "When I left CorpLife, I thought I was leaving behind a world of deceit. Turns out, I was just stepping into a bigger arena."

Sam, with genuine interest: "But you still believe we can make a difference?"

Leo, with a thoughtful nod: "I have to, Sam. Otherwise, what's the point of all this?"

Through these interactions, a mentorship forms. Leo's guidance helps Sam navigate the complexities of their operations, and their bond strengthens over shared ideals and the trials they face.

Meanwhile, Sam's relationship with Ava, the group's spirited artist, takes on a lighter, more humorous tone. Her creative approach to spreading their message often leads to lively debates and moments of much-needed levity.

Ava, presenting her latest piece of art: "What do you think? Subtle enough not to get us arrested but bold enough to make a point?"

Sam, admiring the artwork: "It's... definitely bold. Subtle is debatable."

Their banter reflects a growing camaraderie, a bond forged in the crucible of their shared cause.

However, not all relationships within the group are smooth. Sam occasionally finds himself at odds with Maya, whose intensity and unwavering dedication to the cause sometimes clash with his more cautious approach.

During a heated discussion, Maya challenges Sam: "We can't always play it safe, Sam. Sometimes, you have to take risks to enact change."

Sam, defensively: "I get that, Maya, but we can't help anyone if we're all locked up or worse."

These moments of conflict, while tense, add a layer of realism to the group dynamics. They showcase the diversity of perspectives within the resistance, highlighting that even among those united against a common enemy, disagreements and debates are a natural part of their struggle.

The chapter culminates in a quiet moment between Sam and Lucy, his sister, whose involvement in the resistance first opened his eyes to the realities of their world.

Lucy, in a rare moment of vulnerability: "I'm glad you're here, Sam. I was worried you'd never see the truth."

Sam, with a soft smile: "You were the one who showed me there was a truth to be seen. I'm just sorry it took me so long."

Their conversation underscores the personal nature of Sam's journey. The resistance is more than a cause; it's a collection of individuals, each with their own stories, struggles, and reasons for fighting.

As the chapter closes, Sam's connections within the group have become a vital part of his involvement. These personal bonds not only strengthen his commitment to the cause but also enrich his understanding of what they are fighting for. The resistance, in Sam's eyes, has transformed from an abstract concept into a tangible, human endeavor, driven by relationships as much as ideals.

Unveiling the Plan

Introduction to the Exposé

As Sam becomes more deeply integrated into the resistance, he is brought into the fold of their most ambitious undertaking yet – a daring plan to expose the regime's misdeeds. The group gathers in their hidden headquarters, the air thick with anticipation and anxiety.

Leo, unveiling the plan: "We've managed to get our hands on classified documents. They detail the regime's surveillance tactics and their manipulation of the Social Credit System. It's time the public knew the truth."

Sam's eyes widen in disbelief and excitement. The gravity of what they are about to undertake starts to sink in.

Sam, with a mix of awe and concern: "How did you even get these? What's the plan?"

Leo, with a determined look: "We're going to leak them to the public. But that's not all. We're also planning to hack into the state broadcast system. It's risky, but if we pull it off, everyone will see the reality of what we're living under."

The group discusses the logistics of the plan. The idea is to synchronize the data leak with a disruption of the state's media broadcast, ensuring maximum exposure. It's a plan that requires precision and a bit of luck.

Ava, chiming in with her usual flair: "And for the pièce de résistance, we'll overlay the broadcast with our own message. Think of it as our artistic touch to the revolution."

Sam, half-jokingly, half-nervously: "So, no pressure then? Just hijacking the state media and revealing government secrets. A regular Tuesday night."

Despite the levity, the sense of danger is palpable. They all understand the risks involved – being caught could mean imprisonment or worse.

As the meeting progresses, each member of the group is assigned a role. Sam's knowledge of data analysis makes him key to authenticating the documents and helping with the technical aspects of the broadcast interruption.

Maya, with a nod to Sam: "You're a crucial part of this, Sam. Your skills could be what makes or breaks this whole operation."

Sam, feeling the weight of responsibility: "No pressure, right? Just helping to potentially start a revolution."

The chapter concludes with the group finalizing their plans. Sam feels a mix of fear and exhilaration. He joined the resistance seeking truth, but now he finds himself at the forefront of a significant operation that could change the course of history.

Sam, as he leaves the meeting: "This is it, then. We're really doing this."

The plan to expose the regime's misdeeds marks a turning point in the novel, propelling the narrative from passive resistance to active rebellion. Sam's involvement signifies his transformation from an ordinary citizen to a key player in the resistance's boldest move yet. The chapter ends with a sense of impending action, setting the stage for the dramatic events to come.

Role Assignment

In the thick of their covert operations room, the air buzzing with a mix of excitement and tension, the resistance group begins to assign roles for their ambitious exposé plan. Sam's unique skill set, honed through his years of data analysis, places him in a crucial position.

Leo, addressing the group with a sense of urgency: "We need someone to authenticate the documents we've acquired and help bypass the security protocols of the state broadcast system. Sam, this is where you come in."

Sam feels a surge of adrenaline mixed with a twinge of apprehension. His role is critical to the plan's success, and he understands the weight of the responsibility on his shoulders.

Sam, with a nervous chuckle: "So, basically, I'm the one who gets to crack the code and hopefully not get us all arrested in the process?"

Leo, with a reassuring nod: "Exactly. But you won't be alone. Ava will be your partner in this. Her expertise in digital art and coding will be invaluable."

Ava, with her characteristic wit, chimes in.

Ava, playfully: "Think of us as the dynamic duo of data and disruption. Plus, I've always wanted a sidekick."

Sam, rolling his eyes but smiling: "Great, just what I always wanted. To be a sidekick in a potentially illegal hacking operation."

As they delve into the specifics, Sam's role becomes clearer. He is to work closely with Ava to create a digital 'backdoor' into the state's broadcasting system. His analytical skills will be crucial in navigating the complex security networks and ensuring their message is seen by the masses.

Maya, offering a word of caution: "Remember, timing is everything. We need to coordinate the leak and the broadcast interruption perfectly."

Sam, focusing on the task at hand: "I'll start working on a simulation of their security system. We need to know what we're up against."

The chapter progresses with Sam and Ava working tirelessly, their collaboration marked by moments of intense focus and light-hearted banter. Sam's initial apprehension slowly gives way to a sense of purpose and determination. He's no longer just a bystander in the resistance's activities; he's an active participant making a tangible contribution.

Ava, as they conclude a late-night session: "You're a natural at this, Sam. I'm starting to think you missed your calling as a digital revolutionary."

Sam, exhausted but invigorated: "Let's just hope this revolutionary doesn't end up behind bars."

As the chapter closes, Sam's role in the plan is firmly established. He's integral to the success of their operation, a fact that both terrifies and excites him. His journey from a disillusioned citizen to a key player in the resistance's most daring plan yet is a testament to his growing commitment to their cause. The chapter ends with a sense of anticipation, as the group prepares to take their boldest step yet in exposing the regime's misdeeds.

Preparation and Training

As the resistance's plan inches closer to execution, Sam finds himself immersed in a rigorous regimen of preparation and training, essential for the pivotal role he is to play. The group's hideout, a nondescript warehouse on the city's outskirts, becomes a hub of activity and learning for Sam.

Leo, handing Sam a stack of encrypted data files: "These are past security protocols of the state media system. Study them. Know them inside out. We need to anticipate their moves."

Sam spends his nights poring over the files, familiarizing himself with patterns and vulnerabilities in the system. The task is daunting, but Sam's determination is unwavering.

Sam, during a late-night study session, mutters to himself: "Who knew my love for puzzles would come in handy for hacking government broadcasts?"

Ava joins him, bringing her expertise in coding and digital artistry. Together, they simulate various scenarios, testing out different methods to breach the state's broadcast system.

Ava, as they work through a particularly complex code: "Remember, Sam, in coding and in life, sometimes the most straightforward path is a trap. Think like a hacker, not a data analyst."

Sam, with a smirk: "So, less number-crunching, more cyber-sneaking. Got it."

Their sessions are not just technical but also include lessons in stealth and evasion, taught by Maya, who has experience in covert operations.

Maya, demonstrating a discreet way to pass information: "In our line of work, a simple coffee cup can be the best carrier for data drives. It's all about hiding in plain sight."

Sam, practicing the technique: "I'll never look at my morning coffee the same way again."

As the days pass, Sam's skills sharpen. He learns to communicate through coded messages, to move through the city unnoticed, and to think on his feet – all crucial skills for the impending operation.

The chapter also shows Sam scouting locations to distribute the leaked information, blending into crowds, and observing the daily patterns of potential hotspots.

Sam, to Ava during a scouting mission: "Feels like I'm a spy in some dystopian thriller. If only it were just fiction."

Ava, scanning the area with a practiced eye: "Welcome to our reality, Sam. Just remember, the stakes are real."

The chapter concludes with Sam returning to the warehouse after a successful scouting mission, a sense of accomplishment mixing with the gravity of what lies ahead.

Sam, reflecting on his progress: "A few weeks ago, I was just a guy with a desk job. Now, I'm part of something that could change everything. It's terrifying, but I've never felt more alive."

Through Sam's preparation and training, the chapter highlights his transformation from a reluctant participant to a committed member of the resistance, ready to play his part in the daring plan to unveil the truth. The chapter ends with the group in a final huddle, reviewing their strategy, a moment of calm before the storm of their rebellion.

Emotional and Ethical Challenges

Moral Dilemmas

As the day of the operation draws near, Sam grapples with the moral complexities of his actions. The once-clear lines between right and wrong begin to blur, leaving Sam in a labyrinth of ethical dilemmas.

One evening, in the dim light of their hideout, Sam finds himself in a deep discussion with Leo about the implications of their plan.

Sam, with a troubled expression: "Have you ever thought about the fallout from this? What if innocent people get hurt in the process?"

Leo, pausing thoughtfully before responding: "Every revolution has its casualties, Sam. We can't make an omelet without breaking a few eggs."

Sam, not entirely convinced: "But where do we draw the line? At what point do we become the very thing we're fighting against?"

This conversation marks the beginning of Sam's internal struggle with the ethical implications of their actions. He understands the necessity of their mission, yet he can't shake off the fear of unintended consequences.

Later, as Sam works with Ava on finalizing their digital intrusion into the state broadcast system, he voices another concern.

Sam, hesitantly: "Ava, what if we're wrong about this? What if the information we leak causes more harm than good?"

Ava, focusing on her screen, replies: "I'd rather live with the consequences of action than the regret of inaction, Sam. Sometimes, you have to trust that the truth will lead to the right outcome."

Sam's doubts continue to plague him, even as he recognizes the importance of their mission. The potential risk to innocent bystanders, the ethical ramifications of hacking into a government system, and the personal risk of being identified as a resistor weigh heavily on his conscience.

As the chapter progresses, Sam's interactions with the other group members reveal their own struggles with similar dilemmas. Maya, in a rare moment of vulnerability, shares her own fears.

Maya, quietly confiding in Sam: "I worry about my family. If I'm caught, what happens to them? But then I remember the world I want for them — a world where they're free to speak, to think, to be."

Sam's journey through these moral quandaries adds a rich layer of complexity to his character. It's no longer just a fight against an oppressive regime; it's a battle within himself, between his ideals and the reality of their fight.

The chapter ends with Sam staring out into the night sky, the city lights flickering like distant stars. His reflection in the window mirrors his inner conflict — a man torn between the necessity of action and the weight of its consequences.

Sam, in a whisper to his reflection: "Is this the right thing to do? I guess only time will tell."

In this moment, Sam embodies the emotional and ethical challenges faced by those who dare to rebel against tyranny. His struggles with these dilemmas are a poignant reminder of the human aspect of resistance, the internal battles waged alongside the external fight for freedom and truth.

Strengthening Resolve

Despite grappling with moral dilemmas and the weight of potential consequences, Sam's resolve to contribute to the resistance's cause continues to strengthen. This fortification of spirit is depicted through his interactions with the group and moments of intense personal reflection.

One evening, as the group gathers in their covert meeting space, the tension and gravity of their upcoming operation hang heavily in the air. Sam, although troubled by the ethical implications, finds a sense of clarity and purpose through a conversation with Maya.

Maya, sensing Sam's inner turmoil, says: "It's natural to be afraid, Sam. We all are. But remember why we're doing this. We're not just fighting for ourselves; we're fighting for those who don't have a voice."

Sam, with a newfound sense of determination: "You're right. I can't let my fears hold me back from doing what's necessary. We might be the only hope for change."

In another instance, Sam finds himself in a heart-to-heart with Ava, whose artistic spirit and rebellious energy have always inspired him.

Ava, while they're prepping for the operation: "You know, Sam, in every piece of art I create, there's a piece of rebellion. It's scary, putting it out there, but it's also empowering. Isn't that what we're doing here?"

Sam, reflecting on her words: "Empowerment through rebellion... I like the sound of that. Maybe there's an artist in me yet."

These conversations, coupled with moments of solitude where Sam contemplates his journey, solidify his commitment to the cause. He begins to see beyond the immediate risks and uncertainties, focusing instead on the broader impact of their actions – the potential to ignite a spark of change in a society shrouded in oppression.

Sam, during a moment of reflection: "If we don't stand up to this, who will? It's not just about us; it's about a future where freedom isn't just a word in old books."

As the chapter progresses, Sam's involvement in the planning and execution of their mission becomes more proactive. He starts contributing ideas, drawing from his skills and experiences, and taking on more responsibilities within the group.

Leo, acknowledging Sam's growth during a strategy session: "You've come a long way, Sam. Your insights have been invaluable to us."

Sam, with a modest nod: "I'm just trying to do my part. We all are."

The chapter concludes with Sam looking over the cityscape, a mix of apprehension and resolve in his eyes. The challenges and risks ahead are immense, but his commitment to the resistance, to the ideals of truth and freedom, is unwavering.

Sam, whispering to himself as he gazes out: "This is bigger than any one of us. It's time to make a stand."

Through these interactions and reflections, Sam's character evolves from one of uncertainty and fear to one of resolve and purpose. His journey encapsulates the emotional and ethical challenges inherent in any fight against tyranny, highlighting the transformative power of conviction in the face of adversity. The chapter ends with Sam not just as a member of the resistance but as a driving force within it, ready to face whatever comes next.

Foreshadowing of Risks

As Chapter 3 draws to a close, the narrative takes a darker turn, hinting at the looming risks and potential consequences that Sam and the resistance face in their audacious plan to challenge the regime.

In a tense, late-night meeting, the group gathers to discuss the final details of their operation. The air is thick with a mix of excitement and apprehension. Leo, ever the pragmatist, lays out the stark reality of their situation.

Leo, looking around the room: "We all know what we're up against. The regime won't take kindly to what we're doing. We need to be prepared for the backlash."

Sam, with a sense of foreboding: "You mean when they come after us?"

Leo, nodding solemnly: "Exactly. We're poking a bear, a very powerful, very vindictive bear."

This conversation casts a shadow over the group, bringing into sharp focus the dangers they will soon face. The regime has vast resources and a penchant for ruthlessness, something Sam has only begun to fully grasp.

As the meeting progresses, Maya brings up a recent incident where a known dissident was captured and publicly denounced, a chilling reminder of the regime's methods.

Maya, her voice tinged with concern: "We need to be careful. They're getting better at tracking dissent. Remember what happened to Jackson. We can't afford any slip-ups."

Sam, feeling the weight of her words: "The reality of what we're doing is starting to hit home. It's not just a game; it's life and death."

The chapter culminates in a quiet moment between Sam and Ava, as they finalize their part of the plan. Ava's usually vibrant demeanor is subdued, reflecting the gravity of their undertaking.

Ava, with a rare seriousness: "Sam, whatever happens, I want you to know – it's been an honor fighting with you."

Sam, touched by her words: "Same here, Ava. No matter what, we're in this together."

As Sam leaves the meeting, the streets seem more ominous than usual, the surveillance cameras more menacing. The city that was once his home now feels like a battleground.

The chapter ends with Sam gazing out his apartment window, the skyline a stark contrast to the turmoil brewing within him. The foreshadowing of risks and the potential consequences of their actions hang heavy in the air, setting up a palpable tension for the upcoming chapters.

Sam, whispering to himself: "We're about to change everything. I just hope we're ready for what comes next."

In these final moments, the chapter sets the stage for the high-stakes actions that lie ahead. The resistance's plan, fraught with danger and uncertainty, promises to thrust Sam and his companions into the heart of the conflict, where the risks are as high as the ideals they fight for.

Chapter 4: Under the Watchful Eye

Navigating the Surveillance State

Increasing Awareness

In Chapter 4, 'Under the Watchful Eye,' Sam's acute awareness of the state's pervasive surveillance becomes a central theme. The chapter opens with Sam taking meticulous steps to avoid detection, his every move calculated and deliberate.

As he walks through the bustling city streets, Sam's perception of his surroundings has shifted. He is acutely aware of the surveillance cameras perched on every corner, the drones that intermittently buzz overhead, and the ever-present eyes of the state.

Sam, thinking to himself: "Every step, every action is being recorded. It's like living in a fishbowl, except the water is made of watchful eyes."

Sam has altered his daily routines to avoid patterns that might draw attention. He takes different routes to work, frequents varying cafes, and even alters his appearance slightly.

During a discreet meeting with Ava in a crowded market, they discuss the importance of maintaining this heightened vigilance.

Ava, handing Sam a USB drive hidden inside a book: "You're getting good at this cloak-and-dagger stuff, Sam. Almost didn't recognize you with the hat."

Sam, with a wry smile: "Yeah, well, I figured a little misdirection couldn't hurt. Plus, I've always fancied the mysterious look."

Their conversation is brief and coded, a necessary precaution in a world where words are monitored as closely as actions.

Sam's communication methods have also evolved. He's learned to use encrypted messaging apps, coded language, and even old-fashioned handwritten notes to coordinate with the resistance group. The digital trail he once left without a second thought is now meticulously managed to avoid leaving any breadcrumbs for the state to follow.

In a hidden message to Leo, Sam writes: "The eagle flies at midnight. Location as discussed."

Leo, responding with equal caution: "Confirmed. The nest is ready."

The chapter continues to showcase Sam's increasing adeptness at evading surveillance. He's become skilled at blending into crowds, using public transportation instead of his registered vehicle, and even occasionally donning disguises.

However, this constant state of alertness takes its toll. Sam finds himself perpetually looking over his shoulder, second-guessing every interaction.

During a rare moment of doubt, Sam confides in Maya: "It's exhausting, always being on edge. Sometimes I wonder if it's all worth it."

Maya, with a firm conviction: "It is, Sam. We're fighting for something bigger than ourselves. Remember that."

As the chapter ends, Sam stands in a shadowed alleyway, watching the city's pulse through the lens of his new reality. His life, once an unremarkable tapestry of routine, has transformed into a high-stakes game of cat and mouse with the surveillance state.

Sam, in a moment of reflection: "The more I see, the less I recognize this world. But one thing's clear – I can't go back to the way things were."

The chapter closes on this note of resolve, setting the stage for Sam's continued evolution from a passive citizen to a key player in the resistance, adept at navigating the treacherous waters of the surveillance state.

Close Calls

In 'Under the Watchful Eye,' the constant danger of living under state surveillance is palpably illustrated through a series of close calls that Sam experiences. These incidents underscore the precarious nature of his involvement with the resistance and the ever-present threat posed by the surveillance state.

The first close call occurs when Sam, having altered his route to work, finds himself face-to-face with a random security check. Quick thinking and a stroke of luck allow him to narrowly avoid being stopped.

Sam, recounting the experience to Ava in a low voice: "There I was, face to face with a security drone. I thought it was game over. But then, someone else caught its attention. Never been so grateful for a street performer in my life."

Ava, with a smirk: "Guess it's time to add 'master of evasion' to your resume, Sam."

Another encounter finds Sam in a crowded subway, where he notices a pair of plainclothes officers scanning the crowd. His heart races as he realizes they are looking for someone – potentially him. Using the crowd as cover, he manages to slip away unnoticed, his heart pounding in his chest.

Later, Sam shares the incident with Leo: "It's like playing a game of chess with Big Brother. Every move is a potential checkmate."

Leo, gravely: "You're doing well, but always stay alert. They're getting smarter."

The chapter also describes a tense moment when Sam believes he is being followed. Paranoia grips him as he navigates the labyrinthine streets, trying to lose his potential tail. The realization that any stranger could be an agent of the state is a chilling thought that haunts him.

Sam, during a discreet meeting with Maya: "Every shadow, every face in the crowd could be them. It's getting harder to tell friend from foe."

Maya, understandingly: "The price of resistance, Sam. We live in the shadows to bring light to the truth."

These close encounters with the state's surveillance apparatus serve to heighten the tension and drama of Sam's story. They showcase not only the risks he faces but also his growing skill in evading detection. Each narrow escape reinforces the dangerous game he is playing, a game where the stakes are his life and freedom.

The chapter concludes with Sam returning to his apartment, his nerves frayed but his determination undiminished. The close calls have left him shaken but also more resolved than ever to continue his fight against the regime.

Sam, in a moment of solitude, reflects: "Every close call is a reminder of what we're up against. But I can't let fear stop me. There's too much at stake."

Through these harrowing experiences, Sam's character is further developed, showcasing his courage, resourcefulness, and growing commitment to the cause of the resistance. The chapter ends with an air of suspense and anticipation, as Sam braces himself for the challenges yet to come.

Impact on Personal Life

In 'Under the Watchful Eye,' the strain of Sam's covert activities with the resistance begins to manifest in his personal life. His relationships with family, friends, and colleagues suffer as he becomes increasingly secretive and withdrawn, a necessary shield to protect those he cares about from the dangers of his double life.

The first sign of strain appears in Sam's interactions with his sister, Lucy. Their once easy and open conversations become guarded, as Sam holds back details of his involvement with the resistance for fear of putting her in harm's way.

During a tense phone call with Lucy: "I've just been busy with work, that's all," Sam lies, avoiding her probing questions about his recent absences and distracted demeanor.

Lucy, sensing something amiss, presses: "Sam, you're not just 'busy.' You're distant. You're hiding something. I'm worried about you."

Sam, with a heavy heart: "I'm fine, Lucy. Really. Just... a lot on my mind."

Similarly, Sam's relationship with his friends begins to fray. Invitations to social gatherings are declined, and casual meetups become rare. His once vibrant social life dwindles as he dedicates more time to the resistance, a sacrifice that does not go unnoticed.

A concerned friend, Jenna, confronts him: "You've changed, Sam. You're always so... so evasive now. It's like you're here, but not really."

Sam, struggling to maintain a façade of normalcy: "Just a lot on my plate these days, Jenna. You know how it is."

Even at work, Sam's colleagues notice a shift in his behavior. The once reliable and engaged employee now seems preoccupied, his mind elsewhere.

A coworker, half-jokingly: "What's up with you lately, Sam? Planning a secret getaway? You look like you're plotting to steal the Declaration of Independence or something."

Sam, forcing a laugh: "Yeah, something like that. Just trying to figure things out."

As Sam's life becomes increasingly consumed by his role in the resistance, he realizes the toll it's taking on his personal relationships. The necessity of secrecy, the constant fear of discovery, and the weight of what they are planning to do with the resistance all contribute to a growing sense of isolation.

The chapter closes with Sam sitting alone in his apartment, reflecting on the sacrifices he's making. The fight against the regime, while crucial, is costing him the very connections that once defined his life.

Sam, in a moment of solitude: "Is this what it means to fight for something greater? To lose a part of yourself along the way?"

This internal conflict adds a poignant layer to Sam's character development. His commitment to the cause is unwavering, but it comes at the cost of his relationships and personal happiness. The chapter ends with a sense of melancholy, as Sam grapples with the realization that his involvement in the resistance has irrevocably changed the course of his life.

The Resistance's Covert Operations

Undercover Missions

In 'Under the Watchful Eye,' Sam's involvement with the resistance intensifies as he partakes in a series of undercover missions, crucial to the group's plan to expose the regime. Each operation is fraught with danger, requiring a blend of stealth, cunning, and nerve.

One of Sam's first missions involves meeting with an informant who claims to have insider information about the regime's surveillance technology. The meeting is set in a crowded public park, a place deemed safe enough to avoid suspicion but risky enough to keep Sam on high alert.

Sam, whispering to the informant while pretending to read a newspaper: "So, you're saying the new surveillance drones can identify individuals just by their gait?"

The Informant, glancing around nervously: "Exactly. It's like something out of a sci-fi movie. But you didn't hear it from me."

Another mission sees Sam tasked with acquiring a piece of equipment needed for their planned broadcast intrusion. He finds himself in a dimly lit underground market, a hub for contraband technology.

Vendor, eyeing Sam suspiciously: "This isn't your usual tech store, buddy. What are you looking for?"

Sam, trying to sound casual: "Just a bit of old-school tech. Something to help with a... personal project."

Vendor, with a knowing smirk: "Ah, a 'personal project.' Say no more. Follow me."

Each mission adds another layer to Sam's character, showcasing his adaptability and resourcefulness. He learns to navigate the underbelly of the city, to communicate in code, and to make quick decisions under pressure.

Perhaps the most daring of these operations involves Sam meeting with a disgruntled government employee willing to leak vital information. The rendezvous takes place in a derelict building, away from the prying eyes of surveillance cameras.

Sam, as they exchange a USB drive: "Why are you doing this? Isn't it risky for you?"

Disgruntled Employee, with a bitter laugh: "What's life without a little risk? Besides, I can't stand by and watch what they're doing to us. It's time for some truth."

Through these covert missions, Sam gains not just valuable information and resources for the resistance but also a deeper understanding of the regime's reach and the varied forms of dissent within the city. He encounters individuals from all walks of life, each contributing in their own way to the fight against the regime.

The chapter concludes with Sam returning to the resistance's hideout, a sense of accomplishment mingled with the constant fear of being caught.

Sam, to Leo after completing a mission: "I never knew how many shadows this city had. With each mission, it feels like we're drawing back the curtain a bit more."

These undercover operations are crucial in advancing the resistance's plan and in developing Sam's character from a reluctant participant to a key operative in the struggle against the regime. The chapter ends with an air of anticipation, as the pieces of their grand plan begin to fall into place.

Skills Development

As the covert operations of the resistance intensify in Chapter 4, Sam's journey is marked by the rapid development of new skills, essential for the success of their missions. This progression is crucial not only for the tasks at hand but also for his evolution as a key member of the resistance.

Early in the chapter, a scene unfolds in the resistance's makeshift headquarters, where Ava is teaching Sam the basics of hacking. The atmosphere is intense but sprinkled with Ava's characteristic humor.

Ava, pointing to lines of code on the screen: "Hacking isn't just about breaking into systems. It's about understanding them, knowing their weaknesses."

Sam, focused but overwhelmed: "At this rate, I'll need another ten years before I can even crack a password."

Ava, with a laugh: "Don't worry, you're a natural. Besides, you have me as your teacher. You'll be a master hacker in no time."

In another instance, Sam finds himself practicing the art of stealth and evasion with Maya. They navigate through a crowded market, blending in, unnoticed.

Maya, as they weave through the crowd: "The key is to look like you belong. Confidence is your cloak, anonymity your armor."

Sam, trying to mimic her movements: "I feel more like a clumsy spy in a bad movie."

Maya, with a smirk: "Well, every spy has to start somewhere, right?"

Through these training sessions, Sam also learns the subtle art of social engineering — the skill of manipulating situations and people to gain information or access. Leo becomes his mentor in this complex craft.

Leo, during a mock social engineering exercise: "It's all about reading the person, understanding what makes them tick. People are the best resource and the biggest vulnerability in any system."

Sam, intrigued: "So, it's like being a psychologist and a con artist rolled into one."

Leo, nodding: "Exactly. Use it wisely, and you can unlock more doors than the best hacker."

Each new skill that Sam acquires is soon put to the test in the field. He applies his hacking knowledge to infiltrate a minor government database, his heart racing as he bypasses security protocols under Ava's guidance. His stealth training is tested during a tense operation where he must plant surveillance devices in a government building. And his newfound talent in social engineering proves invaluable when he successfully extracts information from a regime insider during a staged encounter.

The chapter concludes with Sam reflecting on his rapid transformation from an ordinary citizen to a multifaceted resistance operative. He's no longer just a participant in the resistance's activities; he's an instrumental part of their success.

Sam, in a moment of self-reflection: "I've come a long way from the guy who used to analyze data for a living. Now, I'm hacking, sneaking, and manipulating my way to bringing down a regime."

Sam's skills development is a testament to his dedication to the cause and his adaptability in the face of adversity. The chapter ends on a note of accomplishment, but also with the understanding that each new skill brings with it greater risks and challenges.

Building Tension

As the resistance's covert operations escalate in complexity and risk, Chapter 4 artfully builds tension, foreshadowing the major confrontations that lie ahead. Each mission Sam undertakes ratchets up the stakes, pushing him and his companions closer to the edge.

Midway through the chapter, Sam is involved in a risky operation to acquire a crucial piece of equipment from a heavily guarded government facility. The plan requires precise timing and coordination.

In the planning session, Leo cautions: "This isn't like our previous missions. One mistake, and we could all end up in a detention cell."

Sam, acknowledging the risk: "I know the stakes are high. But we need that equipment for the broadcast hack. I'm in."

The operation unfolds with nail-biting tension. Sam and Ava, disguised as maintenance workers, infiltrate the building. Every step they take inside enemy territory amplifies the suspense.

Ava, whispering to Sam as they navigate the corridors: "You know, in a weird way, this is almost exhilarating."

Sam, responding in a hushed tone: "I'll stick with terrifying, thanks. Exhilarating can wait for when we're not in the lion's den."

The mission is successful, but their escape is a close call, leaving the team shaken but more resolved.

As the operations become more daring, the resistance group also begins to feel the strain. The fear of betrayal or a slip-up that could lead to their exposure is a constant companion.

During a debrief, Maya admits: "Every time we go out there, I can't help but think if this will be the day we get caught."

Sam, trying to lighten the mood: "And yet, here we are, still giving the regime a run for their money. We must be doing something right."

Towards the end of the chapter, the resistance undertakes its most audacious operation yet – a coordinated series of hacks into government databases. The plan is to erase records that the regime uses to oppress dissenters.

Sam, as they initiate the hack: "If this works, we could give thousands of people a fresh start, free from the regime's surveillance."

Ava, her fingers flying over the keyboard: "No pressure, right? Just a little digital rebellion."

The operation is fraught with tension, each moment heightening the sense of impending conflict. As the chapter concludes, the group successfully completes the hack, but a chilling message from an unknown source suggests that the regime is closer on their heels than they thought.

The message, displayed on their screen: "We're watching you."

This ominous note underscores the increasing danger of their actions. The chapter ends with Sam and the group realizing that their fight is about to enter a new, more perilous phase, setting the stage for major confrontations in the narrative.

Sam, in a moment of grim determination: "They're onto us. It's only a matter of time now. We need to be ready."

The building tension in this chapter expertly sets the stage for the unfolding drama, with each operation increasing in stakes and suspense, drawing the reader deeper into the world of the resistance and the imminent clash with the regime.

Internal Conflicts and Doubts

Questioning the Cause

In 'Under the Watchful Eye,' as the stakes of the resistance's operations soar, Sam finds himself wrestling with deep-seated doubts about their methods and the potential repercussions of their actions. The internal conflict he experiences adds layers of complexity to his character, showcasing his humanity amidst the chaos of rebellion.

During a moment of quiet reflection after a particularly risky operation, Sam expresses his concerns to Leo.

Sam, voice tinged with uncertainty: "Leo, are we sure we're doing the right thing? What if our actions lead to more harm than good?"

Leo, pausing before responding: "It's a question we all wrestle with, Sam. But remember, inaction has its own consequences. We're fighting against a regime that's strangling our freedom."

Despite Leo's reassurances, Sam's doubts persist. The fine line between liberation and potential anarchy weighs heavily on him.

In another scene, Sam shares his apprehensions with Ava, seeking solace in her usually unwavering resolve.

Sam, confessing his doubts: "Every step we take feels like we're walking on a tightrope. One wrong move, and everything could come crashing down."

Ava, with a rare seriousness in her tone: "I know, Sam. But we can't let fear dictate our actions. We're fighting for a cause, for a future where we're not constantly looking over our shoulders."

Sam's interactions with Maya also reveal his growing internal struggle. Maya, known for her staunch commitment to the cause, challenges Sam's wavering conviction.

Maya, during a heated debate: "You knew what you were signing up for, Sam. We can't afford to second-guess ourselves now."

Sam, defensively: "I'm not saying we should stop. I just... I'm scared of what might happen if we go too far."

As the chapter progresses, the narrative delves deeper into Sam's internal conflicts. His commitment to the resistance is unwavering, but the potential cost of their actions – the possibility of innocent lives being affected, the threat of severe retaliation by the state – casts a shadow over his resolve.

In a moment of solitude, Sam muses aloud to himself: "What's the point of fighting for a free world if our actions lead to more chains, just different ones?"

This introspection culminates in a poignant scene where Sam visits a part of the city heavily impacted by the regime's policies. Seeing the downtrodden faces and the reality of oppression reaffirms his commitment to the cause but also deepens his fears about the path they are on.

Sam, whispering under his breath as he observes the scene: "We're doing this for them, for a better future. But at what cost?"

The chapter ends with Sam more determined yet more conflicted than ever. His journey is emblematic of the moral quandaries faced by those who rise against tyranny. He stands at a crossroads, committed to the resistance's cause but increasingly aware of the ethical and personal toll it entails. The narrative leaves the reader in suspense, pondering the complex choices and potential consequences that lie ahead for Sam and his companions in their fight against the regime.

Emotional Turmoil

Within the fraught atmosphere of Chapter 4, Sam's emotional turmoil takes center stage, revealing the deep-seated fear, guilt, and burden of carrying secrets that come with his role in the resistance. His internal struggle becomes as significant as the external conflict, painting a vivid portrait of a man caught in the throes of a moral and emotional maelstrom.

In a particularly revealing scene, Sam finds himself confiding in Ava in a rare moment of vulnerability.

Sam, his voice laced with weariness: "Sometimes I lie awake at night, haunted by the 'what ifs.' What if we fail? What if I'm making things worse?"

Ava, with a touch of empathy in her usual playful tone: "Sam, you're carrying the weight of the world on your shoulders. Even Atlas would've asked for a break."

The conversation highlights the immense pressure Sam feels, grappling with the potential fallout of their actions on both a personal and a broader societal level.

Another layer of Sam's emotional turmoil is revealed through his interactions with his sister, Lucy. Their once-close relationship has been strained by the secrets Sam must keep, leading to feelings of guilt and isolation.

During a strained phone call with Lucy: "I'm sorry I've been distant, Luce. It's just... work has been crazy," Sam lies, his voice tinged with guilt.

Lucy, her tone a mixture of concern and frustration: "I barely recognize you anymore, Sam. It's like you're there, but you're not really there."

The burden of carrying secrets also manifests in Sam's demeanor at work. He becomes more withdrawn, struggling to maintain a façade of normalcy, which does not go unnoticed by his colleagues.

A concerned coworker, nudging Sam during a coffee break: "You okay, man? You've been looking like a ghost recently. Anything you want to talk about?"

Sam, forcing a smile: "Just haven't been sleeping well. Nothing a good night's rest won't fix."

However, the most poignant depiction of Sam's emotional turmoil comes in a solitary moment, as he reflects on the path he has chosen. The solitude of his apartment amplifies his sense of isolation, the silence speaking louder than words.

Sam, speaking to himself in the mirror: "What have I become? Am I a hero fighting for freedom, or just another pawn in an endless game of power?"

This introspection is interrupted by a sudden realization that his actions, no matter how well-intentioned, could have unforeseen consequences, not just for him but for everyone connected to him.

Sam, in a moment of despair: "I'm in too deep now. There's no turning back, but at what cost?"

The chapter closes with Sam grappling with the complex web of emotions that his involvement with the resistance has woven. Fear, guilt, and the weight of secrets have become his constant companions, each adding to the emotional turmoil that threatens to overwhelm him. This inner conflict adds depth to his character, making him relatable and human, a man caught in a situation much larger than himself, yet bravely facing it each day.

Supportive Interactions

In the midst of his emotional turmoil and internal conflicts, Sam finds moments of solace and reassurance through supportive interactions with other members of the resistance. These exchanges not only alleviate his doubts but also reaffirm his commitment to their cause, showcasing the deep bonds and solidarity within the group.

One such interaction occurs with Leo, who has become a mentor figure to Sam. They find themselves in the resistance's makeshift headquarters after a long day of planning.

Leo, noticing Sam's pensive mood: "You've been quiet today, Sam. Anything on your mind?"

Sam, hesitating before responding: "Just... wondering if we're really making a difference, or if we're just deluding ourselves."

Leo, placing a hand on Sam's shoulder: "We are making a difference, Sam. Every small victory, every piece of information we leak, it's all part of a bigger picture. We're planting seeds of change."

This reassuring conversation helps Sam to see beyond the immediate challenges and focus on the long-term impact of their resistance.

Another moment of support comes from Ava, whose light-hearted demeanor often provides a counterbalance to the gravity of their situation.

During a late-night coding session, Ava quips: "You know, for a guy who spends his days dodging surveillance and hacking into government databases, you sure do brood a lot."

Sam, cracking a smile: "Guess I'm just practicing for my upcoming role as the brooding hero in our resistance saga."

Ava, with a laugh: "Well, you've got the mysterious and tortured part down. Now, you just need a cape."

This playful banter serves as a reminder to Sam that despite the risks and challenges, there is still room for camaraderie and light-heartedness.

Perhaps the most poignant supportive interaction comes from Maya. Known for her steadfast resolve, she shares her own fears and uncertainties with Sam, creating a moment of mutual understanding and solidarity.

Maya, in a rare moment of openness: "I get scared too, Sam. We all do. But I find strength in knowing we're in this together. We're a team, and we have each other's backs."

Sam, feeling a sense of kinship: "Thanks, Maya. It means a lot to know I'm not in this alone."

These supportive interactions play a crucial role in Sam's journey, providing him with the emotional sustenance to continue in the face of adversity. They highlight the importance of human connection and mutual support in a struggle against a seemingly insurmountable foe.

The chapter concludes with Sam feeling more connected to his fellow resistors, their shared experiences and mutual support becoming a source of strength and resolve.

Sam, reflecting on his relationships within the group: "In the darkest of times, it's these bonds that light the way. We're more than just a group fighting for a cause; we're a family."

Through these interactions, the narrative emphasizes the power of collective support and unity in the face of daunting challenges, reinforcing Sam's commitment to the resistance and strengthening his resolve to see their mission through.

Preparations for the Major Exposé

Finalizing the Plan

As Chapter 4 reaches its climax, the focus shifts to the resistance's meticulous final preparations for their major exposé against the regime. The atmosphere is thick with anticipation and a sense of urgency as the group finalizes every detail of their ambitious plan.

n a dimly lit room, the resistance members gather around a cluttered table strewn with maps, digital devices, and a myriad of papers. Leo leads the intricate planning session, his demeanor a mix of intensity and focus.

Leo, pointing to a digital map: "We've got one shot at this. Every step, every second counts. Let's walk through the plan one more time."

Sam, examining the map closely: "The synchronization needs to be perfect. If the broadcast hack and the data leak don't happen simultaneously, it could all fall apart."

Ava interjects, bringing up the technical aspects of their operation.

Ava, scrolling through lines of code on her laptop: "I've set up multiple redundancies for the hack. If one pathway is blocked, we switch to the next. Like a digital game of whack-a-mole."

Sam, with a nervous chuckle: "Comforting to know our fate rests on a game of whack-a-mole."

The group conducts several trial runs, simulating different scenarios and potential hiccups. Maya oversees these drills, ensuring that everyone knows their role and the contingency plans.

Maya, during a trial run: "Remember, if anyone gets compromised, we switch to Plan B. We can't afford any heroics."

Sam, half-serious, half-joking: "Noted. My cape and tights are safely tucked away."

In addition to the technical and strategic preparations, there's also a focus on securing last-minute resources. Sam takes on the task of acquiring additional encryption software from a trusted contact in the underground tech market.

Sam, meeting with the contact in a shadowy alley: "I need the latest in encryption. Something that can give us an edge."

Contact, handing over a small device: "This will make Fort Knox look like a cardboard box. Use it wisely."

As the chapter draws to a close, the resistance members gather for one final meeting. The air is electric with a mix of apprehension and determination.

Leo, addressing the group: "This is it. What we've been working towards. It's going to be risky, but it's our chance to make a real difference."

Sam, looking around at his fellow resistors: "We're ready. Let's bring the truth to light."

The chapter concludes with the group in a collective moment of resolve, their faces a mosaic of courage and resolve. The final preparations for the major exposé have set the stage for a dramatic and potentially transformative event, marking a turning point in their resistance against the regime.

Sam, in a final thought before the operation: "Tomorrow, we change everything. For better or worse, the world won't be the same."

The narrative leaves the reader on the edge of their seat, anticipating the execution of the plan and the repercussions that will undoubtedly follow. Sam's journey, along with his companions in the resistance, has reached a pivotal moment, one that promises to shake the foundations of the dystopian world of 2030.

Role Reaffirmation

As the resistance gears up for their major exposé, Sam's critical role in the operation is reaffirmed, emphasizing both the significance of his contribution and the deep trust the group has placed in him. This section of Chapter 4 solidifies Sam's transformation from a hesitant participant to a key figure within the resistance.

The scene is set in a secluded warehouse, where the group is gathered around an array of screens and equipment. Leo turns to Sam, his expression serious but encouraging.

Leo, addressing Sam directly: "This operation hinges on our ability to breach the state's broadcast system. Sam, you're the linchpin here. We're relying on your skills to pull this off."

Sam, feeling the weight of expectation: "No pressure, then. Just hacking into the most secure system in the state. Piece of cake."

His attempt at humor belies the gravity of the situation, but it's clear that Sam understands the crucial nature of his role.

Ava chimes in, her tone a mix of jest and sincerity.

Ava, playfully nudging Sam: "Hey, no backing out now. You're our resident super-hacker. Plus, I didn't spend all that time training you for nothing."

Sam, with a wry smile: "Guess it's too late to ask for a raise, huh?"

As the preparations continue, Maya approaches Sam, her demeanor reflecting the respect and trust she has developed for him.

Maya, sincerely: "Sam, I know we've had our differences, but I want you to know – I have complete faith in you. We all do."

Sam, nodding appreciatively: "Thanks, Maya. That means a lot. I won't let you guys down."

In another poignant moment, Sam and Leo work side by side, fine-tuning the final elements of their plan. Leo's mentorship has been instrumental in Sam's development, and this moment highlights the bond they have formed.

Leo, as they work: "When this is all over, Sam, you're going to have quite the story to tell. Just make sure it has a happy ending, okay?"

Sam, with determination in his voice: "I'll do my best. After all, every good story needs a hero, right?"

The reaffirmation of Sam's role underlines not just his technical skills but also the personal growth he has undergone since joining the resistance. He has become more than just a member; he is a symbol of the trust and camaraderie that binds the group together.

The chapter concludes with Sam taking a moment to reflect on his journey. He looks around at his fellow resistors, feeling a sense of belonging and purpose.

Sam, in a moment of introspection: "This is more than just a mission. It's a testament to what we can achieve when we stand together. I'm ready."

Sam's role reaffirmation sets the stage for the upcoming exposé, highlighting his integral place in the resistance's most daring operation yet. The chapter ends with a sense of anticipation and unity, as the group prepares to take a stand against the oppressive regime.

Anticipation and Anxiety

As Chapter 4 draws to a close, the atmosphere among Sam and his fellow resistance members is thick with a potent mix of anticipation and anxiety. They are on the cusp of their most significant and risky operation yet, and the air is electric with the tension of what is to come.

In the final hours before the operation, the group gathers in their hidden headquarters, making last-minute checks and going over the plan one more time. The seriousness of the situation is palpable, and each member is acutely aware of the stakes.

Sam, looking over the equipment and software: "Feels like we're about to jump out of a plane without knowing if our parachutes will open."

Ava, with a nervous laugh: "Well, Sam, let's just hope we're good at free falling. Or at least landing."

Despite the attempt at humor, there's an undercurrent of apprehension in her voice, shared by everyone in the room.

Leo steps forward, his expression solemn as he addresses the group, his eyes lingering on Sam.

Leo: "This is it. Everything we've worked for leads to this moment. Remember, stay sharp, stick to the plan, and watch each other's backs."

Sam, taking a deep breath: "We've got one chance at this. Let's make it count."

As they finalize their preparations, Maya comes over to Sam, placing a reassuring hand on his shoulder.

Maya: "We're all in this together, Sam. No matter what happens out there, I'm proud of what we've accomplished."

Sam, nodding in agreement: "Together till the end. For freedom, for truth."

The chapter concludes with the group in a final huddle, a moment of unity before they embark on their perilous mission. The tension in the room is a tangible force, a mixture of fear and determination.

Sam, looking around at his companions: "It's been an honor to stand with all of you. Let's go change the world."

As they break the huddle and move to their respective positions, the anticipation and anxiety reach a crescendo. The chapter ends with Sam stepping out into the night, the weight of the upcoming operation heavy on his shoulders, yet bolstered by the solidarity of his comrades.

This closing scene sets the stage for the high-stakes action to unfold in the following chapters, leaving the reader on the edge of their seat, eager to see how Sam and the resistance's bold plan will play out in their fight against the oppressive regime of 2030.

Chapter 5: The Brink of Change

Execution of the Exposé

D-Day Arrives

Chapter 5, titled 'The Brink of Change,' opens with the resistance group in the throes of final preparations for their monumental exposé. The air is thick with a concoction of tension, anticipation, and a sense of impending change.

The scene is set in a dimly lit, abandoned factory that has become the nerve center for the operation. Sam and his companions are busy with last-minute checks, each member focused on their crucial role in the impending plan. The tension in the room is palpable, a tangible representation of the stakes at hand.

Sam, double-checking the encryption on their broadcast signal: "If this encryption doesn't hold, we might as well send a direct invitation to the regime's doorstep."

Ava, working alongside him, tries to inject a bit of levity: "Well, if we do end up getting caught, I hope they at least appreciate the effort we put into this."

Leo, ever the composed leader, oversees the final preparations, his demeanor a blend of calm and stern focus.

Leo, addressing the group: "Remember, once we start this, there's no turning back. We need to be ready for anything."

The emotional state of the group is a mix of determination and underlying fear. Each member knows the risks involved but is committed to the cause.

Maya, checking her communication device, adds: "We knew this day would come. It's time to show the world the truth."

Sam feels the weight of the moment as he oversees the final technical setup. The responsibility he carries is immense, and his usual composure is tinged with a hint of nervousness.

Sam, to himself: "This is it. No more rehearsals, no more planning. It's showtime."

As the clock ticks down to the launch of their operation, there's a moment where Sam exchanges glances with each of his fellow resistors. In their eyes, he sees not only the resolve to fight for freedom but also the silent acknowledgment of the potential cost of their actions.

Sam, rallying the group: "We all know what we're up against. Let's make sure our message is heard loud and clear. For freedom."

The chapter concludes with the group taking their positions, each member engaging in their part of the plan. The factory, once silent and still, buzzes with the energy of a group poised to change the course of history.

As they initiate the first phase of their exposé, the tension peaks, leaving readers on the edge of their seats, waiting to see how the operation unfolds.

Sam, as he initiates the broadcast hack: "Here goes nothing... or maybe everything."

The opening of Chapter 5 sets the stage for a dramatic sequence of events, as the resistance embarks on their most daring endeavor yet. The mood is one of high stakes and heightened emotions, marking the beginning of a chapter that promises to be a turning point in the story.

The Protagonist's Role

In 'The Brink of Change,' the spotlight falls on Sam as he undertakes a pivotal role in the execution of the resistance's exposé. His task, critical and fraught with danger, involves broadcasting the message that will unveil the regime's dark secrets to the world.

As the moment of truth approaches, Sam is stationed at a makeshift broadcasting hub, a labyrinth of wires, screens, and digital equipment surrounding him. The tension is almost palpable as he prepares to infiltrate the state's broadcasting system, a feat that requires precision, skill, and a good dose of courage.

Sam, focusing intently on his computer screen, mutters: "It's now or never. Time to dance with the devil in the digital realm."

Ava, who is assisting Sam, adds with a hint of nervous humor: "Just make sure you lead. I hear the devil's got two left feet."

Sam's fingers fly over the keyboard as he navigates through layers of security encryption. The rest of the group watches anxiously, understanding that the success of their entire operation hinges on this moment.

Leo, watching over Sam's shoulder: "You're doing great, Sam. Just a little bit further."

Sam, half-joking, half-serious: "No pressure, right? Just hacking into the most secure broadcast system in the state."

Finally, with a few final keystrokes, Sam successfully breaches the system. A wave of relief mixed with triumph washes over him as he initiates the broadcast of their pre-recorded message, exposing the regime's misdeeds.

Sam, exhaling deeply: "We're in. The truth is on its way."

As the message begins to air across various channels, the group braces for the impact it will have. Sam's role doesn't end with the hack; he remains on high alert, ready to counter any attempts by the regime to cut off their broadcast.

Ava, as they watch the message spread: "Look at that, Sam. You just turned the state's propaganda machine into our personal megaphone."

Sam, a mix of satisfaction and apprehension in his voice: "Let's hope it's loud enough to wake the city up."

The chapter culminates with Sam monitoring the broadcast, ensuring it reaches as many people as possible. His role in the operation not only showcases his technical prowess but also his growth as a character — from a reluctant participant to a key player in the resistance's most daring action yet.

Sam, as the broadcast continues uninterrupted: "This is it. We've done our part. Now it's up to the people."

Sam's role in the execution of the exposé sets the stage for the dramatic unfolding of events, leaving readers eagerly anticipating the impact of the resistance's bold move against the dystopian regime of 2030.

Execution in Detail

In 'The Brink of Change,' the execution of the resistance's daring exposé unfolds with gripping detail, as seen through Sam's perspective. Each step of the plan is meticulously described, revealing the challenges and setbacks they encounter, which demand quick thinking and adaptation.

The action kicks off with Sam initiating the hack into the state's broadcasting system. His screen glows with lines of code, his fingers dancing over the keyboard in a rhythmic frenzy.

Sam, focusing intently: "Here goes. Bypassing the first firewall now."

Ava, monitoring a secondary screen: "You've got incoming traffic. Looks like they've detected the breach."

Sam, without missing a beat: "Rerouting through a proxy server. Keep an eye on that traffic."

As Sam navigates through the digital defenses, the tension mounts. Each hurdle he overcomes is met with another challenge, a digital game of cat and mouse that keeps the reader on the edge of their seat.

Meanwhile, other members of the group are positioned across the city, ready to disseminate additional information and counter any propaganda the regime might deploy in response.

Over the radio, Leo's voice comes through: "Teams in position across the city. We're ready to amplify the message."

Sam, responding while still focused on his screen: "Good. The broadcast is going live in 3... 2... 1..."

With a final keystroke, Sam breaks through the last barrier, and their pre-recorded message begins to air across the city's various media channels. However, their victory is short-lived as they encounter a significant setback.

Ava, alarmed: "Sam, we've got a problem. They're jamming the signal."

Sam, his calm demeanor faltering: "Already? Okay, time for Plan B. I'm switching to the backup frequency."

In a race against time, Sam works furiously to restore their broadcast, his fingers a blur across the keyboard. The group's message flickers back to life on the screens, but it's a tenuous hold.

Maya, through the radio: "We're getting responses across the city. People are seeing it, Sam. Keep it going!"

Amidst the chaos, Sam's resolve strengthens. He deftly counters each attempt by the regime to shut down their broadcast, his adaptability and quick thinking keeping their message alive.

Sam, breathing heavily from the exertion: "This is like playing whack-a-mole on a city-wide scale. But we've got this."

As the chapter nears its end, the intensity reaches a fever pitch. The group's message is spreading, but so is the regime's response. The streets buzz with activity, both from regime forces and from citizens responding to the exposé.

Sam, as he continues to maintain the broadcast: "No matter what happens next, we've started something that can't be stopped."

The chapter concludes with Sam and the group bracing for the regime's countermeasures, their message echoing through the city. The detailed execution of their plan, fraught with challenges and setbacks, showcases not only Sam's technical expertise but also the resistance's collective determination to fight for truth and freedom.

The narrative leaves readers in suspense, wondering how the regime will react and what the consequences will be for Sam and his companions. The stage is set for a dramatic continuation, as the impact of their actions begins to ripple through the dystopian world of 2030.

Public Revelation

Broadcasting the Truth

In 'The Brink of Change,' a pivotal moment arrives as the resistance successfully broadcasts the truth to the public, piercing through the veil of the regime's propaganda. This section vividly depicts the scene as the truth is disseminated in various forms, from hacked broadcasts to viral digital messages.

The scene opens with Sam and Ava in their makeshift broadcasting hub, surrounded by screens displaying different channels across the city. With Sam's hacking skills and Ava's digital expertise, they break through the state-controlled media, replacing the usual propaganda with their pre-recorded exposé.

Sam, as the broadcast goes live: "And... we're on. Let's see how they like a dose of reality for a change."

Ava, watching the screens intently: "Look at that, Sam. Our message is all over the city. It's actually working!"

On the streets, leaflets with the same information begin to circulate, handed out by other members of the resistance. People gather in small groups, reading the leaflets, their expressions a mix of shock and disbelief.

A passerby, reading a leaflet: "Is this for real? Have we been lied to all this time?"

Another, joining in: "It looks like it. I can't believe it... but it all makes sense now."

Online, the resistance's message goes viral, spreading like wildfire across social media platforms and digital forums. Sam's handiwork ensures that the message bypasses the regime's digital censorship, reaching a wide audience.

On a digital forum, a user comments: "Everyone needs to see this. It's time for the truth to come out."

Another user responds: "Sharing this everywhere. They can't hide the truth any longer."

In homes across the city, families watch in astonishment as their regular programming is interrupted by the resistance's broadcast. The revelation of the regime's misdeeds and manipulation is laid bare for all to see.

In one household, a shocked viewer exclaims: "This can't be happening. How could they do this to us?"

A family member, equally stunned, adds: "We've been living in a lie. It's all coming out now."

The chapter captures the range of reactions from the public – shock, anger, disbelief, and for some, a dawning sense of empowerment. The truth, long hidden and suppressed, is now in the open, sparking conversations and debates across the city.

Sam, watching the reactions from their hub: "This is it, Ava. We've started something big. There's no turning back now."

Ava, with a mix of pride and apprehension: "Yeah, we've lit the fuse. Let's hope we're ready for the explosion."

The chapter concludes with the city abuzz with the revelations, setting the stage for a dramatic shift in the narrative. The successful broadcasting of the truth marks a turning point in the resistance's fight against the regime, igniting a flame of awareness and potential uprising among the populace. The story leaves readers in suspense, eager to see how this newfound knowledge will reshape the dystopian world of 2030.

Mixed Reactions

As the truth about the regime's misdeeds is broadcast across the city, Chapter 5 of 'The Brink of Change' vividly captures the spectrum of public reactions, ranging from shock and disbelief to anger and, in some instances, realization and support.

The first reaction is seen in a bustling café, where patrons are initially caught off guard by the sudden change in their usual programming. The café goes silent as the exposé plays on the screen.

A stunned customer, spilling his coffee: "What in the world is this? Is this some kind of prank?"

The barista, equally shocked, responds: "Doesn't look like any prank to me. That's some heavy stuff they're showing."

In a residential area, a group of neighbors gathers around a television in the local community center. As the reality of the information sinks in, the initial shock gives way to anger.

An older resident, shaking his head in disbelief: "All these years, we've been fed lies. How could they do this to us?"

A young woman, clenching her fists: "We need to do something. We can't let them get away with this!"

On social media platforms, the reactions are instantaneous and varied. Some express skepticism and disbelief, while others voice their support and call for action.

A social media post reads: "Can't believe what I'm seeing. Is this really happening? #RegimeLiesExposed"

Another user replies: "We need to stand up and demand answers. It's time for change! #TruthPrevails"

In a local park, a group of teenagers watching the broadcast on their phones discusses the revelations with a mix of cynicism and hope.

Teenager 1, skeptically: "Do you think this is legit? I mean, it could be some elaborate hoax."

Teenager 2, more optimistic: "I don't know, it feels real. And if it is, maybe it's the wake-up call we needed."

Meanwhile, in a corporate office, employees watch the broadcast, leading to heated discussions about the implications of the revelations.

One employee, visibly upset: "This changes everything. How can we continue to work under a regime like this?"

Her colleague, pondering the situation: "It's not just about work. It's about our whole way of life. We've been living in a bubble."

The chapter illustrates the diverse reactions through the lens of different segments of society, reflecting the complex web of emotions and thoughts that the truth unleashes. From disbelief and shock to a burgeoning sense of empowerment, the public's response is a mosaic of the human experience in the face of groundbreaking revelations.

The narrative ends on a note of uncertainty and potential, as the public grapples with the newly exposed reality, setting the stage for societal shifts and the possible rise of a collective movement for change.

Sam, witnessing the reactions, reflects: "We've opened Pandora's box. Now we have to face whatever comes out of it."

Immediate Fallout

As the revelations from the resistance's exposé ripple through the city, 'The Brink of Change' delves into the immediate and tense response from the authorities. The regime, caught off guard by the sudden dissemination of the truth, scrambles to regain control, leading to a series of reactive measures.

The first response is an aggressive attempt to shut down the broadcast. In the control room, Sam and Ava work frantically to keep their signal alive as they face digital attacks from the regime's cybersecurity forces.

Ava, as she counters a hacking attempt: "Looks like we've got company. They're trying to jam the signal."

Sam, focused on his screen: "Not on my watch. Rerouting the feed now."

Meanwhile, on the streets, propaganda vans and digital billboards that were hijacked by the resistance start flickering, as the regime tries to regain control of their broadcasting network.

In an attempt to discredit the information, state-controlled media outlets begin airing their counter-narrative. On television screens, a regime spokesperson addresses the public.

Regime Spokesperson, with a calm demeanor: "Do not be swayed by these baseless accusations and doctored footage. These are the actions of radicals who aim to destabilize our society."

On the other hand, the regime's response is not limited to digital warfare. There are immediate moves to retaliate against the resistance. Security forces are dispatched to suspected resistance hideouts, leading to tense chase scenes in the city.

Over the resistance's communication channel, Maya's voice is urgent: "We've got regime troops on our tail. Everyone, initiate evasion protocols now!"

The chapter paints a vivid picture of the chaos ensuing in the city. While the public grapples with the shock of the revelations, the regime is in damage control mode, its authority and credibility shaken.

In one particularly harrowing scene, Sam and a group of resistors narrowly escape a raid on one of their hideouts.

Sam, as they flee through a back alley: "That was too close. We need to stay one step ahead of them."

The immediate fallout from the exposé is a whirlwind of action and reaction, with the regime desperately trying to quash the uprising of truth. The resistance, though under immense pressure, remains determined to keep the momentum going.

The chapter concludes with the regime's spokesperson making a veiled threat on state television, hinting at severe consequences for those involved in the resistance's actions.

Regime Spokesperson, sternly: "Those responsible for spreading falsehoods and inciting unrest will be found and brought to justice."

This ending sets a foreboding tone, suggesting a looming escalation in the conflict between the regime and the resistance, with Sam and his companions firmly in the crosshairs of authority. The narrative leaves the reader in suspense, wondering how the resistance will continue their fight under the increasing pressure of the regime's retaliation.

Confrontation and Sacrifice

Confrontation with Authorities

In the heart-pounding chapter of 'The Brink of Change,' a direct and intense confrontation unfolds between Sam, his fellow resistance members, and the state forces. This clash, marked by a high-speed chase and a dramatic standoff, escalates the narrative tension to new heights.

The confrontation begins when Sam and a small team of resistors are ambushed by state security while distributing additional evidence in a densely populated area of the city. Suddenly, armored vehicles block their escape routes, and armed forces converge on their location.

Sam, realizing they're cornered, shouts: "Scatter! We can't let them catch us all!"

Ava, as she darts into an alleyway: "Great, just what I needed today – a workout chased by goons in gear!"

The scene shifts to a heart-stopping chase through the narrow, winding streets of the city. Sam and his companions use their knowledge of the urban landscape to their advantage, but the state forces are relentless.

During the chase, Maya, communicating via earpiece: "Sam, we're trying to divert some of them your way. Hang tight!"

Sam, dodging through back alleys: "Define 'hang tight' in this context, Maya!"

Despite their efforts, Sam and a fellow resistor, Jacob, find themselves trapped in a dead-end alley. Facing a squadron of state enforcers, the tension in the air is electric.

Jacob, brandishing a makeshift weapon: "Looks like we're doing this the hard way."

Sam, taking a defensive stance: "I preferred the easy way, but here we are."

The standoff is intense, with Sam and Jacob desperately fighting off the encroaching forces. Just when it seems they're about to be overwhelmed, a sudden distraction allows them a narrow window of escape.

In a daring and selfless act, Jacob draws the attention of the enforcers, sacrificing his chance of escape to give Sam an opportunity to flee.

Jacob, yelling to Sam: "Go, Sam! Get the truth out there!"

Sam, reluctant to leave his comrade behind: "Jacob, come on!"

Jacob, with a determined look: "It's the only way! Make it count!"

Sam, with a heavy heart, uses the diversion to slip away, the sounds of the confrontation echoing behind him. This moment of sacrifice is a poignant reminder of the high stakes they are playing for.

The chapter ends with Sam escaping into the labyrinthine city, his mind racing with the implications of Jacob's sacrifice and the unresolved confrontation. The narrative leaves the reader in suspense, wondering what the consequences of this confrontation will be and how Sam will continue the fight in the face of such personal loss.

Sacrifice

As the narrative of 'The Brink of Change' reaches a critical juncture, Sam is faced with a heart-wrenching decision, leading to a significant personal sacrifice for the greater good. This moment encapsulates the essence of his journey, marking a turning point in his character development.

After the harrowing confrontation with the state forces and Jacob's selfless act to ensure his escape, Sam finds himself at a crossroads. He knows that the information they have is vital for the public, but also that broadcasting it puts him in imminent danger.

As Sam regroups with the remaining members of the resistance, including Ava and Leo, they face the stark reality of their situation.

Ava, looking gravely at Sam: "We've got one last batch of evidence. But it's going to be a suicide mission to broadcast it."

Sam, with a mixture of determination and sorrow: "Then it's my turn to step up. Jacob bought us this chance. I won't let his sacrifice be in vain."

Leo, understanding the gravity of Sam's decision, places a hand on his shoulder.

Leo: "You don't have to do this, Sam. We can find another way."

Sam, shaking his head: "No. This is the only way. It's what I signed up for. What we all signed up for."

With the final piece of evidence in hand, Sam sets out to the broadcasting hub, a move that will undoubtedly draw the attention of the regime. It's a perilous journey, and Sam is acutely aware that it might be his last.

Sam, to Ava before leaving: "Take care of the others, Ava. Keep the fight going."

Ava, her eyes glistening with unshed tears: "You're one hell of a guy, Sam. Be careful out there."

Sam's journey through the city is tense and fraught with danger. He uses all the skills he has learned, evading patrols and surveillance cameras. But as he nears the hub, he realizes he's being followed. In a final act of defiance, Sam decides to broadcast the evidence right there, in the open, knowing full well it will lead to his capture.

Sam, as he starts the broadcast, whispers to himself: "For truth, for freedom. For all of us."

The chapter ends with Sam successfully transmitting the last batch of evidence, just as the regime's forces close in on him. As he is apprehended, his last glimpse is of the evidence playing on the screens across the city – his sacrifice ensuring the truth is revealed.

Sam, as he's being led away, a hint of a smile on his face: "It's out there now. No turning back."

This sacrifice, made by Sam for the greater good, is a powerful testament to his character's growth and commitment to the cause. The chapter leaves the reader with a mix of sadness and admiration for Sam's bravery, setting a poignant tone for the chapters to follow.

Emotional Impact

In the aftermath of Sam's courageous sacrifice, 'The Brink of Change' delves into the profound emotional repercussions on both Sam and his fellow resistance members. This section poignantly captures the collective sense of loss, the palpable uncertainty, and the unwavering determination that rises from the ashes of sacrifice.

Following his capture, the narrative shifts to Sam in confinement. Alone in his cell, he grapples with a maelstrom of emotions. Despite the direness of his situation, there's a lingering sense of satisfaction from having successfully broadcast the truth.

Sam, in a moment of introspection: "They can lock me up, but they can't imprison the truth. It's out there now, beyond their reach."

Meanwhile, the emotional toll on the other members of the resistance is palpable. Ava, Leo, and the others gather, the mood somber as they come to terms with Sam's capture.

Ava, her voice tinged with sadness: "Sam did what he thought was right. He knew the risks, but it doesn't make this any easier."

Leo, with a heavy heart: "He's one of the bravest people I've known. We owe it to him to keep fighting, to make sure his sacrifice wasn't in vain."

The group is visibly shaken, but there's a newfound resolve among them. Sam's sacrifice becomes a rallying point, a symbol of their commitment to the cause.

Maya, her determination renewed: "This is far from over. We need to regroup, plan our next move. Sam's sacrifice has lit a fire in the hearts of the city."

In the city, word of Sam's capture and his act of defiance spreads, fueling a mix of outrage and inspiration among the populace. Sam's sacrifice becomes a catalyst, sparking discussions and clandestine meetings.

A scene in a crowded café, where patrons are discussing the recent events:

Patron 1: "Did you hear about that guy, Sam? Broadcast the truth right under the regime's nose!"

Patron 2, with a mix of admiration and concern: "Yeah, a real hero. But now he's in their hands. Makes you wonder what they'll do to him."

The chapter closes with a focus on Sam in his cell, his thoughts turning to his fellow resistors and the uncertain future that lies ahead.

Sam, gazing out of a small window in his cell: "Keep the fight going, guys. This is just the beginning."

The emotional impact of Sam's sacrifice resonates deeply, leaving an indelible mark on the narrative. It's a poignant exploration of the personal cost of rebellion and the unyielding spirit of those who fight for change. The chapter sets a tone of resolve amidst adversity, moving the story forward into uncharted territory.

End with Uncertainty

Uncertain Future

As 'The Brink of Change' reaches its conclusion, the narrative pivots to a scene of profound uncertainty for Sam and the remaining members of the resistance. Despite their success in revealing the truth to the public, the future remains shrouded in ambiguity, with the repercussions of their actions and the state's impending response hanging heavily in the air.

In a clandestine meeting following Sam's capture, the atmosphere among the resistance members is tense yet defiant. They have achieved their immediate goal, but at a significant cost. The uncertainty of what comes next looms large.

Ava, her voice laced with concern: "We've opened the eyes of the city, but what now? What does this mean for all of us, for Sam?"

Leo, gazing thoughtfully at the group: "We've started a movement, but the regime won't take this lying down. We need to be prepared for whatever they throw at us next."

The conversation shifts to speculation about the state's next moves. Will they crack down harder, or will the public's newfound awareness lead to change?

Maya, with a steely resolve: "We knew the risks when we started this. Now it's about staying one step ahead, keeping the momentum going."

The chapter then cuts to Sam in his holding cell, portraying his solitary contemplation. Despite the grimness of his situation, there's a sense of hope that flickers in his thoughts.

Sam, to himself: "This isn't the end. It's just the beginning of something bigger. They can't stop the truth now."

In the city, citizens are seen in various settings, digesting the revelations. Some are fearful of the regime's retaliation, while others are emboldened to speak out. The city is a tinderbox of emotions, a reflection of the uncertainty that permeates the air.

In a crowded market, two vendors converse:

Vendor 1: "Do you think things will change now?"

Vendor 2, with a shrug: "Hard to say. But at least now we know the truth. That's got to count for something."

The chapter concludes with a panoramic view of the city at dusk. The streets are alive with whispered conversations and furtive glances, a city on the brink of something yet unknown.

Narrative closing: "In the heart of the city, under the watchful eyes of the regime, a spark has been lit. Where it leads, only time will tell. But one thing is certain – the world of 2030 will never be the same again."

This final scene encapsulates the uncertainty that defines the chapter's end. The resistance, though successful in their immediate goal, faces an unpredictable future, their actions a catalyst for change, the extent of which remains to be seen. The chapter leaves the reader in suspense, pondering the possibilities and consequences that lie ahead in this transformed world.

Reflecting on Actions

n the final moments of 'The Brink of Change,' Sam finds himself in the solitary confines of a regime holding cell, where he engages in a profound reflection on his actions and their far-reaching impact. This contemplative scene provides a window into his thoughts, as he ponders the aftermath of the resistance's bold move and what the uncertain future might hold.

Alone, with only the dim light of his cell for company, Sam's mind races through the events that led him here. He replays the broadcast, the public's reaction, and the frantic escape that followed. Despite the grimness of his situation, there's a sense of quiet pride in what they have achieved.

Sam, whispering to himself: "We did it. We got the truth out there. But at what cost?"

His thoughts are interrupted by the faint echoes of guards outside his cell, a stark reminder of the regime's power. Sam realizes the gravity of the situation, not just for himself, but for the entire resistance and the city at large.

Sam, contemplating his fate: "They might have me locked up, but the ideas we've unleashed, they can't be contained. I just hope the others are safe."

As he sits in the dim light, Sam's thoughts turn to the future. The uncertainty of what lies ahead is daunting, but there's a glimmer of hope that their actions have sparked a change, a ripple that could grow into a wave of resistance.

Sam, with a mixture of doubt and hope: "Have we started a revolution, or just a fleeting moment of defiance? Only time will tell."

The chapter closes with Sam looking out of the small window in his cell, the city skyline visible in the distance. It's a city on the edge of change, its future as uncertain as his own.

Sam, gazing out: "Whatever happens next, I've played my part. The city won't forget what we've shown them. The seeds of change have been sown."

This reflective scene serves as a powerful conclusion to the chapter, leaving readers with a sense of both completion and anticipation. Sam's internal monologue underscores the complexity of their struggle against the dystopian regime and sets the tone for the ongoing narrative, filled with uncertainty but also a glimmer of hope for what the future might hold.

Setting Up for the Next Phase

As Chapter 5 of 'The Brink of Change' draws to a close, the narrative artfully provides a sense of closure to the current phase of the resistance's plan while simultaneously leaving the door ajar for the next stage of their struggle. This section masterfully balances resolution with anticipation, setting the stage for the unfolding story.

In the resistance's hidden base, the remaining members - Ava, Leo, Maya, and others - gather around a dimly lit table, their faces etched with a mixture of fatigue and determination. The successful broadcast of the truth has marked the end of one chapter in their fight, but they are acutely aware that their struggle is far from over.

Leo, addressing the group: "We've done what we set out to do, but this is just the beginning. The regime will come back at us harder now. We need to be ready."

Ava, with a wry smile: "Well, nobody said starting a revolution would be easy. Guess it's time to plan our next act of defiance."

The conversation shifts to strategizing for the future. They discuss potential moves, aware that the dynamics of their fight have changed. The city is buzzing with a newfound awareness, and the regime is on the defensive.

Maya, her eyes fierce with resolve: "We've ignited a spark. Now we need to fan the flames. It's time to mobilize the people, turn this into a movement."

The chapter then cuts back to Sam in his cell. He's deep in thought, aware that his comrades are continuing the fight without him. His spirit remains unbroken, and he takes solace in the knowledge that he played a crucial role in awakening the city.

Sam, murmuring to himself: "Keep the fight going, guys. I may be down, but I'm not out. Not as long as the resistance lives on."

The final moments of the chapter show a montage of scenes across the city - whispered conversations in cafes, clandestine meetings in shadowed alleys, and graffiti messages of defiance appearing on walls. The public, once passive, is now stirred, and the seeds of rebellion are taking root.

The chapter ends with a return to the resistance base, where the group is huddled around a makeshift map of the city, plotting their next move.

Ava, pointing to the map: "There are pockets of support all over the city. We need to connect them, give them a unified voice."

Leo, nodding in agreement: "The next phase begins. We'll need all the allies we can get."

This ending leaves the reader with a sense of both completion and anticipation. The resistance has achieved a significant victory, but the road ahead is fraught with challenges. The story thus sets up for the next phase of the struggle, promising more action, more challenges, and the continued fight for freedom in the dystopian world of 2030.

Chapter 6: A Shaken World

Aftermath of the Revelation

Immediate Impact

Chapter 6, 'A Shaken World,' opens with a vivid portrayal of the immediate aftermath following the exposé by the resistance. The city is engulfed in a whirlwind of chaos and confusion, affecting both the general public and the corridors of power.

The chapter begins in the heart of the city, where crowds gather around screens, still displaying the remnants of the resistance's broadcast. The revelation of the regime's misdeeds has left the populace in a state of shock, their expressions ranging from disbelief to anger.

On a busy street corner, a flabbergasted citizen exclaims to his friend: "Can you believe what they were hiding from us? It's like we've been living in a lie!"

The friend, equally stunned, replies: "I know, it's all coming undone. But what do we do now? It's not like we can just go back to normal after this."

In the higher echelons of the regime, there's a palpable sense of panic and urgency. Officials scramble to formulate a response, their usual air of control replaced with frenzied activity.

Inside a regime office, an official frantically speaks on a phone: "We need to contain this, now! Get our PR team on it. And find out who's behind this broadcast!"

Meanwhile, the resistance members watch the unfolding events from their hidden base, their faces a mix of anxiety and hope. They knew their actions would create waves, but the sheer scale of the public's reaction is both exhilarating and daunting.

Ava, watching the news feeds: "Look at this, the whole city's talking about it. We've really stirred the hornet's nest."

Leo, with a cautious tone: "This is just the start. We've got the regime on the back foot, but they'll strike back hard. We need to be ready."

On the streets, impromptu debates and discussions break out among citizens. The revelation has triggered a widespread questioning of the status quo, with people from all walks of life contemplating what this means for their future.

In a crowded café, a group of young people heatedly discuss:

Young Person 1: "This is our chance, right? To demand change, to take back control."

Young Person 2, more skeptical: "It's not going to be that easy. The regime won't just sit back and let us overturn everything."

The chapter captures the essence of a society on the brink of transformation. The once unchallenged authority of the regime is now being questioned, while the general populace grapples with the realization of having been deceived for so long.

The chapter ends with a city in turmoil, its future uncertain but its people awakened. The resistance's broadcast has not just revealed the truth; it has ignited a spark of change that cannot be easily extinguished.

Narrative closing: "In the wake of revelation, a city finds itself at a crossroads. The path ahead is uncharted, the outcome uncertain. But one thing is clear – the world as they knew it has been irrevocably shaken."

Government Response

In 'A Shaken World,' the narrative shifts to focus on the government's desperate attempts to regain control in the wake of the resistance's explosive revelations. This section of the chapter details the regime's multifaceted response, which includes harsh crackdowns, disinformation campaigns, and emergency broadcasts aimed at countering the narrative set forth by the resistance.

The chapter portrays scenes of regime officials in a state of heightened urgency. In a secure government facility, high-ranking officers and propaganda experts convene in a hastily arranged meeting to strategize their response.

A senior official, addressing the room: "We need to act fast. Launch a counter-campaign. Discredit the resistance's claims. Control the narrative."

A propaganda specialist, chiming in: "We'll need a mix of fear and reassurance. Remind the people why they need us. And paint these rebels as the enemies of peace."

On the streets, the regime's response manifests as a visible increase in security. Patrols are doubled, checkpoints are set up, and dissent is swiftly and ruthlessly quashed. The heavy hand of the regime is felt across the city, as they attempt to stamp out any sparks of rebellion.

At a checkpoint, a regime officer barks orders: "Check everyone! No exceptions. We can't let these troublemakers undermine our authority."

Meanwhile, the regime launches an emergency broadcast, seeking to reassure the public while subtly sowing seeds of doubt about the resistance.

On every screen across the city, a regime spokesperson declares: "Citizens, do not be swayed by the baseless accusations of a few radicals. We are working tirelessly to ensure your safety and prosperity."

In quieter corners of the city, rumors swirl and debates rage. While some citizens buy into the regime's narrative, others see through the façade.

In a dimly lit bar, patrons watch the broadcast with skepticism:

Patron 1, cynically: "Here we go, the same old song and dance. 'Trust us, we know what's best.'"

Patron 2, more hopeful: "But people have seen the truth now. How many will keep drinking the regime's Kool-Aid?"

The chapter paints a picture of a regime in crisis mode, scrambling to maintain its grip on power. Their efforts to control the narrative are met with varying degrees of success, creating a tense atmosphere of uncertainty and defiance.

Narrative closing: "As the regime tightens its grasp, the city holds its breath. In the battle for the truth, every word becomes a weapon, every silence a statement. The struggle for the soul of the city intensifies, with each side vying to write the next chapter of its history."

Public Uprising

As 'A Shaken World' progresses, the narrative vividly captures the burgeoning public uprising in response to the revelations by the resistance. This section of the chapter depicts various segments of the populace beginning to question and challenge the regime, resulting in protests, debates, and a general sense of unrest sweeping across the city.

In a bustling urban square, a spontaneous protest erupts, with citizens holding makeshift signs and chanting slogans inspired by the resistance's broadcast. The air is charged with a newfound sense of empowerment and defiance.

A passionate protester, shouting to the crowd: "No more lies! No more control! We demand the truth!"

Another protester, joining in: "It's our city! Our lives! Time for change!"

The scene shifts to a local university where students gather, engaging in heated debates about the regime's legitimacy and the resistance's revelations. The youth, once apathetic, are now at the forefront of questioning the status quo.

A student, animatedly speaking in a debate: "We've been fed propaganda our whole lives. It's time we think for ourselves, question everything."

Her classmate, skeptically: "But can we really trust these so-called revelations? What if it's just another power play?"

In quieter residential areas, groups of neighbors meet in secret, discussing the implications of the revelations and what it means for their future. The atmosphere is one of fear, hope, and determination.

In a hushed living room, a resident whispers: "We can't just sit back anymore. The truth is out there. We have to do something."

Another resident, cautiously: "But we have to be careful. The regime won't take this lying down. We need to be smart about it."

Meanwhile, graffiti and street art reflecting the resistance's message begin to appear across the city, turning public spaces into canvases of dissent and expression.

A graffiti artist, spray-painting a mural, says to his friend: "Let's see them try to silence these walls."

The friend, keeping watch, replies: "You're going to get us arrested, but I gotta admit, it's worth it."

The chapter skillfully portrays a city on the brink of transformation. The once submissive public is now awakening, their voices growing louder and more confident. The regime's grip on power is beginning to loosen as the seeds of dissent and demand for change take root.

Narrative closing: "In the shadow of revelation, a city finds its voice. From the echoes of defiance in the streets to the whispered conversations behind closed doors, the people of the city are waking up. A new chapter is being written, one of courage, unity, and an unquenchable thirst for change."

The Protagonist's New Reality

Personal Consequences

In 'The Protagonist's New Reality,' Chapter 6 of 'A Shaken World' delves into the profound personal consequences Sam faces following his daring actions and sacrifice. Captured by the regime, Sam confronts a new, harsh reality defined by isolation, the pain of loss, and the constant threat of betrayal.

The chapter opens with Sam in a dim, confined cell, a stark contrast to the world he once navigated as a free member of the resistance. He grapples with the harsh reality of his situation, the silence of the cell punctuated by his own thoughts.

Sam, reflecting aloud in his cell: "Well, this is a fine mess you've gotten yourself into, Sam. Broadcast the truth and win a one-way ticket to the regime's hospitality suite."

Despite his attempt at humor, the weight of his situation is evident. Sam is haunted by the memory of Jacob's sacrifice, the image of his friend's brave act playing over in his mind.

Sam, whispering to himself: "Jacob, I hope your spirit is free, even if I'm not. You didn't deserve this end."

Sam's solitude is interrupted by the occasional visit from an interrogator, probing for information about the resistance. The threat of betrayal hangs over these interactions, as Sam must navigate the delicate balance between self-preservation and loyalty to the cause.

During an interrogation, the interrogator insinuates: "Your friends aren't coming for you, Sam. But you can still save yourself. Give us something to work with."

Sam, with a defiant yet weary tone: "Sorry to disappoint, but my memory's a bit foggy these days. Must be the charming ambiance in here."

As the chapter progresses, Sam's resilience is tested. The isolation takes its toll, and he clings to the memories of the resistance's achievements and the hope that his actions have ignited a spark for change.

Sam, in a moment of solitude: "We shook the world, even if I can't see it from this cell. That has to count for something."

The narrative paints a poignant picture of Sam's predicament. Once an active participant in the resistance, he now faces the consequences of his actions from the confines of a cell. His sacrifice has become both his burden and his legacy.

Narrative closing: "In the stillness of his cell, Sam finds strength in the echoes of the past and the whispers of a future he helped to awaken. Though confined, his spirit remains unbroken, a silent testament to the enduring power of truth and resistance."

The chapter ends with Sam staring at the small window in his cell, a sliver of the outside world visible, symbolizing the hope that persists even in the bleakest of circumstances. The story leaves the reader contemplating the personal cost of rebellion and the indomitable nature of the human spirit.

Changed Perception

In 'The Protagonist's New Reality,' a key focus of Chapter 6 is on how Sam's perception of the world and the resistance has evolved. Confined in a regime cell, Sam undergoes a journey of introspection, experiencing moments of doubt, guilt, and ultimately, a reaffirmation of his beliefs.

The chapter portrays Sam grappling with the new reality of his isolation. The once active and driven member of the resistance now finds himself questioning the impact of his actions and the path he chose.

Sam, in a moment of self-reflection: "Did we really make a difference, or just poke the bear? All this, for what?"

His thoughts are interrupted by the distant sound of protests and unrest outside, a reminder of the turmoil his actions helped ignite.

Sam, perking up slightly at the distant noise: "At least the city's awake. That's something, right?"

Amidst his solitude, Sam battles with feelings of guilt, particularly about the fate of his comrades like Jacob.

Sam, whispering to the walls: "Jacob, I'm sorry. I wish I could have done things differently. You deserved better."

However, as the chapter progresses, Sam's reflections lead to a gradual reaffirmation of his beliefs. He starts to recognize the broader impact of his and the resistance's actions.

Sam, with a growing sense of resolve: "We sparked a fire. A fire the regime can't extinguish. That has to mean something."

His change in perception is further fueled by a stealthy visit from a resistance member posing as a janitor. The brief interaction provides Sam with a much-needed connection to the outside world and the resistance's ongoing efforts.

Resistance Member, whispering: "Your message got through, Sam. The city's rising. Don't lose hope."

Sam, his spirits lifted: "Tell them... tell them to keep fighting. It's far from over."

The chapter concludes with Sam, now more determined and resolute, gazing through his cell window. The sight of a distant protest, a small but visible flame in the night, reminds him that his sacrifice was not in vain.

Narrative closing: "In the quiet of his cell, Sam's doubts give way to conviction. The world he knew has changed, and so has he. With a renewed sense of purpose, he holds onto the belief that out of the chaos he helped create, a better world can emerge."

This section of the chapter effectively illustrates the profound transformation in Sam's perspective. His journey of self-questioning leads to a deeper understanding of the resistance's role and the significance of their fight against the regime, setting the stage for his continued impact on the unfolding events.

Evolving Role

In 'The Protagonist's New Reality' of 'A Shaken World,' Chapter 6 explores the evolving role of Sam within the resistance, despite his confinement. Cut off from direct action, Sam's role undergoes a transformation as he adapts to contribute to the cause in a new capacity.

The chapter reveals how Sam, once a hands-on operative, now becomes an emblem of inspiration and a strategist from within his cell. Utilizing clandestine communications with the outside world, he starts influencing the resistance's strategies and offering guidance based on his insights.

During a covert conversation with Ava, who visits disguised as a janitor:

Sam, whispering through the cell bars: "Ava, you need to keep the momentum going. Use the public's unrest to our advantage."

Ava, nodding subtly: "We're trying, Sam. But it's not the same without you out here. You always had a knack for this."

Sam, with a hint of humor in his grave situation: "Turns out, prison gives you a lot of time to think. Use that. Stir the pot, but be smart about it."

Despite his physical confinement, Sam's influence within the resistance grows. His messages, passed through secret notes or whispered exchanges, begin to shape the group's tactics.

In a meeting with other resistance members, Ava conveys Sam's suggestions.

Ava, relaying Sam's message: "Sam says we should focus on information warfare now. Keep spreading the truth, make it harder for the regime to lie."

Leo, considering the advice: "He's right. Sam may be behind bars, but his mind is still our best weapon."

Sam's evolving role also involves becoming a symbol of the resistance's resilience and determination. Stories of his sacrifice and continued defiance spread among the populace, fueling the movement's spirit.

In a hushed gathering of resistance members, a young recruit speaks:

Young Recruit: "Even locked up, Sam's still fighting. If he can do that, so can we. He's not just a person anymore; he's a symbol of our struggle."

The chapter concludes with Sam in his cell, reflecting on his new role in the resistance. He understands that while he can no longer be on the front lines, his contributions are still vital.

Sam, alone with his thoughts: "I may be caged, but my spirit isn't. As long as I can still think, still inspire, I'm still in the fight."

This section of the chapter powerfully illustrates how Sam's role within the resistance evolves to meet the challenges of their new reality. His transition from an active operative to a strategist and symbol of hope highlights the fluid nature of roles within a movement and the diverse ways individuals can contribute to a cause.

Shifting Societal Dynamics

Fractured Society

In the section titled 'Fractured Society' of Chapter 6, 'A Shaken World,' the narrative vividly captures the diverse and often conflicting reactions rippling through society following the resistance's exposé. This section delves into the complexities of a society in flux, highlighting the varied responses from different groups – from outright denial to vehement opposition, and the many who find themselves in a state of confusion and uncertainty.

The chapter opens in a luxurious part of the city, where the elite and regime loyalists gather. Their conversations reveal a mix of denial and unwavering support for the regime.

At a high-end social club, one loyalist scoffs: "This so-called exposé is nothing but rebel propaganda. The regime has kept us safe and prosperous."

Another, sipping an expensive drink, adds: "Exactly. A few malcontents can't be allowed to disrupt our way of life."

Conversely, in another part of the city, there are pockets of society where anger and opposition are brewing. Community centers and local bars become hotbeds of anti-regime sentiment.

In a crowded bar, a fiery patron declares: "It's all out in the open now! We can't let them get away with this. It's time to stand up!"

Her friend, nodding in agreement: "Right. We've been blind for too long. This regime's days are numbered."

Amidst these polarized views, a significant portion of the populace finds themselves grappling with confusion and uncertainty. The revelations have shaken their trust in the regime, but the fear of change and the unknown holds them back.

In a suburban neighborhood, a group of neighbors discusses the recent events:

Neighbor 1, anxiously: "I don't know what to believe anymore. Can we really trust these rebels?"

Neighbor 2, equally uncertain: "I'm not sure, but can we afford to ignore what they've shown us? It's all so overwhelming."

The chapter skillfully portrays the fractured nature of society in the wake of the revelations. As the regime's narrative unravels, so too does the societal cohesion it had enforced, leading to a city divided in its perceptions and responses.

Narrative closing: "In a city now awakened to unsettling truths, the fabric of society begins to fray. Lines are drawn, allegiances tested, and the once monolithic support for the regime starts to crumble. In every corner of the city, from the gleaming towers to the shadowed alleyways, the people face a choice – to cling to the familiar or to brave the winds of change."

This portrayal of a society grappling with newfound truths and divided in its response sets the stage for further developments in the story, reflecting the complexity and unpredictability of societal change.

Emergence of New Alliances

In 'Shifting Societal Dynamics,' a crucial part of Chapter 6, the narrative unfolds to reveal the emergence of new alliances and factions within the society and the resistance, spurred by the protagonist's actions and the regime's exposé. These new alliances include unexpected defectors from the government and grassroots groups inspired by the resistance's courage.

The chapter introduces a scene in a dimly lit underground meeting place, where a former government official, now a defector, meets with key members of the resistance.

Ava, eyeing the defector warily: "So, you expect us to just trust you? Yesterday you were on their side."

The Defector, earnestly: "I can't be a part of their lies anymore. I have information, and I want to help."

Leo, cautious but intrigued: "Alright, let's hear what you've got. But remember, we're watching you."

This scene sets the tone for a new dynamic within the resistance, as they cautiously navigate alliances with former enemies who bring valuable insights and resources.

Elsewhere in the city, inspired by Sam's actions and the truth revealed, grassroots groups begin to form, galvanized into action. These groups range from intellectual circles hosting clandestine discussions to more active organizations planning protests.

In a secret meeting of a newly formed group:

Group Leader: "Sam's sacrifice showed us it's possible to stand up to the regime. We need to organize, spread the message."

A new member, full of zeal: "Yeah, it's time to take the fight to the streets. Let's make sure Sam's voice echoes in every corner of the city!"

The chapter also highlights the challenges these new alliances face, from internal disagreements to the ever-present threat of regime crackdowns. The resistance must navigate these waters carefully, balancing their need for new allies with the risk of infiltration.

Back at the resistance base, Ava expresses concern:

Ava: "These new groups and defectors could be valuable, but they could also be our downfall if we're not careful."

Leo, contemplating the chessboard before him: "It's a risk, but one we have to take. We're stronger together. Sam knew that, and so do we."

The emergence of these new alliances and factions paints a picture of a society in transformation, a world where the black-and-white lines of allegiance are blurred, and new shades of resistance emerge.

Narrative closing: "In the shadow of upheaval, new bonds are forged, and unlikely alliances take shape. The landscape of resistance is changing, growing more diverse and complex, mirroring the multifaceted nature of the society it seeks to redefine. In this new reality, the seeds of change sown by Sam and his comrades begin to bear fruit, signaling the dawn of a new era in the fight for truth and freedom."

This section of the chapter emphasizes the evolving nature of the resistance and the society as a whole, setting the stage for further developments and deeper exploration of the changing dynamics in the world of 2030.

Increasing Tension

In 'Shifting Societal Dynamics,' a significant portion of Chapter 6, 'A Shaken World,' is dedicated to illustrating the escalating tension between the regime and its growing number of detractors. This segment of the narrative expertly sets the stage for potential conflicts and escalations, emphasizing the volatile atmosphere pervading the city.

The chapter depicts a series of tense confrontations and standoffs across the city. In one such scene, a group of regime enforcers faces off against a crowd of peaceful protesters. The air is thick with anticipation and fear.

A regime enforcer, shouting through a megaphone: "Disperse immediately! This assembly is illegal under regime laws."

A bold protester, standing firm: "We're not afraid anymore! You can't silence us all!"

In the corridors of power, the regime's officials hold emergency meetings, their frustration and anxiety palpable. They are aware that their grip on the populace is weakening.

In a dimly lit government office, a high-ranking official states: "These rebels are becoming a real thorn in our side. We need to crack down, before this gets out of hand."

Another official, nervously pacing: "But the more we push, the more they resist. It's like trying to stamp out a fire that keeps spreading."

Meanwhile, the resistance, bolstered by new alliances, is energized by the public's growing support. They hold clandestine strategy sessions, planning their next moves.

Leo, addressing the group: "The regime is getting desperate; we can use that to our advantage. But we need to be smart, stay one step ahead."

Ava, with a touch of sarcasm: "Well, if we're taking requests, I'd like to not end up in a cell next to Sam. Just for variety's sake."

The chapter also captures moments of tension within the resistance itself, as they navigate the complexities of their expanded coalition and differing viewpoints.

A new member, passionately: "We need to take more direct action. Show the regime we're not just a bunch of talkers."

Maya, cautioning: "Easy there. We can't just rush into things. That's what the regime expects."

The narrative crescendos with a series of small but significant acts of defiance across the city, from graffiti to impromptu speeches, symbolizing the growing unrest and the populace's hunger for change.

Narrative closing: "In a city on the brink, every word, every action, holds the weight of potential revolution. The streets become a chessboard of move and countermove, with the regime and the resistance locked in a tense dance of wills. As the tension mounts, the city holds its breath, waiting for the spark that could ignite the powder keg of rebellion."

This section of the chapter effectively builds on the atmosphere of increasing tension, creating a sense of impending conflict that keeps the reader engaged and anticipating what might come next in the unfolding drama of 2030.

Reflection and Regrouping

Quiet Reflection

In 'Reflection and Regrouping,' the final section of Chapter 6, 'A Shaken World,' the narrative takes a poignant turn, providing a moment of quiet reflection for the protagonist, Sam, and other key characters. Amidst the turmoil and escalating tensions, these scenes allow for a deeper exploration of their emotions, offering insights into their internal struggles, moments of mourning, celebration of small victories, and contemplation of their next moves.

In his cell, Sam finds a rare moment of solitude to reflect on the journey so far. The walls of his cell, though confining, can't contain his thoughts, which roam freely, revisiting past actions and contemplating the future.

Sam, speaking softly to himself: "We've come so far, yet the road ahead seems longer than ever. Jacob, I wish you could see the seeds we've sown."

Meanwhile, in a safe house, Ava and Leo gather with other members of the resistance. They share a moment of respite, acknowledging the small victories they have achieved despite the overwhelming odds.

Ava, raising a makeshift toast: "To us, the stubborn few who dare to dream of a better world."

Leo, with a wry smile: "And to those we've lost along the way. May their memories fuel our fight."

The scene shifts to Maya, who finds herself on a secluded rooftop, gazing at the city's skyline. The chaos of the streets below seems distant as she allows herself a moment of contemplation.

Maya, whispering to the stars: "What would you do, Sam? How do we keep this flame burning?"

In these moments of reflection, each character confronts their own doubts and fears, but also reaffirms their commitment to the cause. The quiet introspection serves as a counterpoint to the action and uncertainty that define their daily existence.

Back in his cell, Sam comes to a realization: "This isn't just my fight anymore. It's ours. Together, we're stronger."

The chapter concludes with a sense of collective resolve among the characters. Despite the challenges and losses, they find strength in their shared purpose and in the small moments of connection and reflection.

Narrative closing: "In the stillness of the night, each in their own way, the resistance finds solace in reflection. Their journey is fraught with peril, but in these quiet moments, they find the strength to continue. The fight for freedom, for truth, for a new dawn, goes on."

This section of the chapter poignantly captures the resilience of the human spirit in the face of adversity, setting the stage for the ongoing struggle and the unwavering determination of the protagonists.

Strategic Planning

In the 'Reflection and Regrouping' section of 'A Shaken World,' Chapter 6 culminates with the resistance regrouping and engaging in strategic planning. Faced with the regime's aggressive countermeasures and a rapidly evolving landscape, they gather to adapt their strategies and plan their next steps in this high-stakes game of rebellion.

The scene is set in a dimly-lit basement, serving as the current headquarters for the resistance. Around an old table strewn with maps and digital devices, key members of the resistance, including Ava, Leo, and Maya, gather to chart their course forward.

Ava, scanning the maps: "The regime's cracking down hard. We need to be smarter, stay under their radar."

Leo, his eyes fixed on a digital screen: "Agreed. It's time for guerrilla tactics. Hit and run, spread our message, keep them guessing."

The group discusses potential targets for their next operations — propaganda centers, data hubs, and other strategic points that could weaken the regime's grip on the city.

Maya, pointing to a location on the map: "What about this media hub? If we can hack into it, we could broadcast our message city-wide."

Ava, with a hint of sarcasm: "Sure, because our last broadcast went so smoothly. Let's just send out invitations to our next one."

Despite the levity, there's a sense of urgency in their planning. They are acutely aware that the regime is adapting to their tactics, necessitating a constant evolution of their own methods.

Leo, looking up from the map: "We also need to consider alliances. The underground networks, the defectors... anyone who can add to our strength."

The conversation shifts to Sam and his continued influence despite his imprisonment. His actions have inspired new tactics and a renewed determination within the resistance.

Ava, reflecting on Sam's impact: "Sam might be locked up, but he's still with us. We carry his spirit in every move we make."

The chapter ends with the group finalizing their plans, a mix of determination and caution coloring their approach. They understand that the path ahead is fraught with danger, but the stakes are too high to back down now.

Narrative closing: "In the shadows of the regime's towering presence, the resistance plots its next moves. With each strategy, each decision, they weave the fabric of a new future, one thread at a time. In the heart of the city, a quiet yet relentless revolution continues to grow, fueled by strategy, bravery, and the undying hope for a free world."

This section poignantly captures the resilience and adaptability of the resistance, setting the stage for the unfolding drama in the chapters to come.

End with Anticipation

As 'Reflection and Regrouping' concludes in Chapter 6 of 'A Shaken World,' the narrative crescendos to a close with a palpable sense of anticipation. This segment expertly sets the stage for upcoming events, hinting at a looming large-scale conflict, significant shifts in the resistance's strategy, and the potential for unexpected twists in the unfolding narrative.

In the dimly-lit resistance headquarters, after finalizing their strategic plans, the members share a moment of tense anticipation. The air is charged with a mix of apprehension and determination as they prepare for what might be their most daring operation yet.

Ava, looking around the room: "This is it, isn't it? The big play. Feels like everything's been leading up to this moment."

Leo, nodding gravely: "Yes. We've set things in motion that we can't stop now. This is where we either make our mark or fall trying."

As the group disperses, there's a shared understanding that the coming days will be critical. The city, already on the edge, seems to be teetering towards a decisive moment that could change everything.

Maya, as she gathers her things: "Whatever happens, we've started something that can't be undone. Sam's sacrifice won't be in vain."

The scene transitions to a quiet rooftop where Ava stands alone, gazing at the city skyline. Her expression is one of contemplation, mixed with a resolve that reflects the gravity of their situation.

Ava, to herself: "Alright, Sam, you got us here. Now it's on us to finish what you started. Hope you're ready for a show."

The chapter concludes with an unexpected development: a regime insider covertly contacts the resistance, offering critical information. This unexpected alliance adds a new layer of complexity and potential to the resistance's plans.

In a hushed phone call, the Insider whispers: "I have information that could change everything. But we must act quickly."

Leo, responding with cautious intrigue: "We're listening."

This final scene leaves the reader on the edge of their seat, brimming with anticipation for the next chapter. The resistance is poised on the brink of a pivotal moment, their actions potentially set to alter the course of the city's future.

Narrative closing: "As the city sleeps, a storm brews on the horizon. In the quiet before the dawn, the resistance braces for the coming day, a day that could herald the dawn of a new era or the dusk of their bravest dreams. The stage is set, the players ready, and the city waits with bated breath for the curtain to rise on the next act of its tumultuous history."

This ending encapsulates the heightened sense of anticipation for what's to come, setting up a tantalizing premise for the subsequent developments in this gripping tale of resistance and rebellion.

Chapter 7: Reflections and Realizations

The New Phase of Resistance

Adapted Strategies

In 'The New Phase of Resistance,' the opening section of Chapter 7, 'Reflections and Realizations,' the narrative dives into the evolving tactics of the resistance as they adapt to the shifting landscape. The protagonist, Sam, though confined, plays a crucial role in this evolution, his influence felt even from behind the walls of his cell.

The chapter begins in the clandestine depths of the resistance's new base of operations. The atmosphere is one of intense focus and quiet urgency as the group discusses their adapted strategies in response to the regime's increasing crackdown.

Ava, outlining a new plan: "With the streets crawling with regime forces, it's time we go deeper underground. Hit-and-run tactics, keep them guessing."

Leo, nodding in agreement: "Agreed. We also need to strengthen our network. More allies mean more eyes and ears."

Despite his imprisonment, Sam continues to influence the resistance's strategies. Through smuggled messages and secret communications, his insights and ideas permeate the group's planning.

In a whispered conversation during a covert visit to Sam's cell:

Maya, passing a hidden note to Sam: "We need your insight, Sam. The game has changed."

Sam, with a wry smile despite his situation: "Never thought I'd be masterminding a revolution from a cell. But here we are. Tell Ava and Leo to stay nimble, stay smart."

: Resisting the New World Order

The resistance also explores new alliances, reaching out to sympathetic individuals within the regime and other underground factions. This expansion brings a new set of challenges and opportunities.

In a secret meeting with a potential ally from within the regime:

Potential Ally: "I can get you information, but it's risky. What's in it for me?"

Ava, cautious but opportunistic: "A chance to be on the right side of history. And trust me, we're excellent at keeping secrets."

As the chapter progresses, it showcases the resistance's shift to more covert operations, employing guerilla tactics, and disseminating underground propaganda to counter the regime's narrative.

Leo, during a strategy session: "It's time we take the fight to the digital realm. We can't outgun them, but we can outsmart them."

The narrative paints a picture of a resistance in flux, adapting to the ever-changing dynamics of their struggle against the regime. Sam's role as a strategist from his cell adds a layer of complexity to the group's operations.

Narrative closing: "In the shadows of the city, the resistance reshapes itself, morphing to meet the challenges of a new day. With each adapted strategy, each covert operation, they write a new chapter in their fight for freedom, a chapter marked by cunning, resilience, and an unwavering commitment to their cause."

This section of the chapter sets the tone for the new phase of resistance, one that is more clandestine and strategic, showcasing the adaptability and determination of Sam and his fellow resistors.

Increased Stakes

In the 'The New Phase of Resistance' segment of Chapter 7, 'Reflections and Realizations,' the story delves into the heightened stakes and escalating risks facing the resistance. As the regime becomes more desperate and brutal in its efforts to maintain control, the resistance is compelled to undertake increasingly perilous missions and make difficult choices.

The chapter opens in a dimly-lit safe house, where members of the resistance gather to discuss their latest intelligence on the regime's activities. The air is thick with tension, reflecting the gravity of their situation.

Ava, reviewing a report: "Looks like the regime is ramping up their surveillance. They're getting desperate."

Leo, with a hint of sarcasm: "Desperate regimes and their toys. Maybe they'll finally upgrade from those antique surveillance cams."

Despite the levity, the group is acutely aware of the increased danger. Every move they make is fraught with risk, and every decision could have dire consequences.

Maya, weighing in: "We need to be extra careful. The regime's crackdowns are getting more violent. Our next move could be our riskiest yet."

The chapter showcases a particularly daring mission where the resistance attempts to intercept critical information from a regime convoy. The operation is fraught with danger, requiring meticulous planning and precise execution.

During the planning session:

Ava, outlining the mission: "We hit the convoy here and extract the data. Timing has to be perfect."

A new recruit, nervously: "And if we're caught?"

Leo, with a wry smile: "Let's just say we won't be around for their hospitality."

As the resistance embarks on the mission, the narrative captures the intensity and danger of their endeavor. They navigate through the city's underbelly, evading regime patrols and surveillance drones.

In the midst of the operation, Maya whispers into her comms: "Convoy in sight. Everyone, on your marks."

Ava, from a lookout point: "And let's hope we live to brag about this one."

The mission, while successful, comes at a cost. A close brush with regime forces leaves the group shaken, underlining the perilous nature of their fight.

After the mission, back at the safe house, the group reflects on their close call:

Ava, visibly shaken: "That was too close. We got the intel, but we can't keep relying on luck."

Leo, solemnly: "Luck, skill, whatever it takes. We knew what we signed up for."

The chapter closes with the group processing the implications of their increasing risks. They understand that as the stakes rise, so must their resolve and ingenuity.

Narrative closing: "In the darkened corners of the city, where the resistance plots its next move, the air is heavy with the weight of increased stakes. Each step forward is a dance with danger, a gamble against the regime's tightening grip. But even as the shadows grow deeper, the flame of rebellion burns brighter, fueled by the courage and determination of those who dare to dream of a free world."

This section of the chapter skillfully highlights the escalating stakes for the resistance, setting up an atmosphere of suspense and anticipation for the challenges they will face in their continued struggle against the regime.

Philosophical and Ethical Musings

Contemplation on Freedom

In the 'Philosophical and Ethical Musings' section of Chapter 7, 'Reflections and Realizations,' the narrative deepens as it explores the protagonist's reflections on the concepts of freedom, control, and human responsibility under the shadow of an oppressive regime. Sam, confined yet contemplative, engages in profound introspection and dialogues, pondering the intricate and often paradoxical nature of these themes.

In a scene set in his cell, Sam finds himself lost in thought, gazing at the small streak of light filtering through his window. His internal monologue reveals a man wrestling with complex philosophical questions.

Sam, thinking to himself: "They've got me locked up, but what about the others out there? Are they truly free, or just in a larger cell, blinded by the illusion of control?"

During a rare visit from Ava, disguised as a custodian, their conversation steers towards the nature of freedom and its cost.

Ava, in a hushed tone: "We're fighting for freedom, Sam. But sometimes, I wonder... what does that even mean in a world like ours?"

Sam, with a sigh: "Freedom... it's more than just the absence of chains. It's the power to choose, to act. But with that power comes responsibility, a price not everyone's willing to pay."

In another scene, as Sam overhears the guards discussing the state of the city, he reflects on the regime's iron grip and the populace's awakening.

Sam, overhearing the guards: "You can control people through fear, but you can't control their thoughts, their hopes. That's where true power lies."

Sam's musings are juxtaposed with scenes from the outside world, where the resistance and ordinary citizens grapple with their newfound awareness. These vignettes provide a canvas for Sam's thoughts, illustrating the tangible impact of these philosophical concepts in action.

In a crowded market, an overheard conversation:

Citizen 1, pondering: "Ever since the truth came out, I've been thinking. We've been puppets for so long. What does it mean to really be free?"

Citizen 2, thoughtfully: "Freedom's not just doing what you want, I guess. It's about making choices that count, standing up for what's right."

As the chapter progresses, Sam's reflections evolve into a deeper understanding of the resistance's role and the collective responsibility in the fight for freedom.

Sam, in a moment of clarity: "Freedom isn't just an ideal to strive for; it's a perpetual struggle, a constant choice to stand against those who would take it away."

The chapter concludes with Sam, despite his confinement, finding a sense of purpose in his philosophical journey, understanding that his struggle and that of the resistance are pivotal in shaping the future of freedom in their world.

Narrative closing: "In the stillness of his cell, Sam's thoughts transcend the physical barriers around him. His musings on freedom become a beacon, illuminating the path for those still fighting in the shadows. In a world marred by control and oppression, these reflections serve as a reminder of the enduring human spirit's quest for true freedom."

This section poignantly captures the protagonist's philosophical journey, offering a deep and introspective look at the themes of freedom and responsibility, which are central to the narrative and resonate profoundly with the ongoing struggle against the regime.

The Cost of Rebellion

In the 'Philosophical and Ethical Musings' section of Chapter 7, 'Reflections and Realizations,' the narrative delves into the moral and ethical cost of the rebellion. Through dialogues and introspections, it explores the themes of sacrifice, the greater good, and the personal toll of engaging in a prolonged fight for a cause.

A poignant scene unfolds in the resistance's makeshift headquarters, where Ava and Leo engage in a candid conversation about the cost of their struggle.

Ava, looking at a wall filled with photos of fallen comrades: "Every face here tells a story. A story of sacrifice. But was it worth it?"

Leo, somberly: "We've sparked change, inspired hope. But the price... sometimes, I wonder if we really understood the cost when we started this."

This dialogue segues into a reflection on the broader impact of their actions, weighing the victories against the losses.

Ava, with a heavy heart: "We've shaken the regime, but at what cost? Families torn apart, lives lost..."

Leo, resolutely: "But we've given people something to believe in. Isn't that worth fighting for?"

In a contrasting scene, Sam, alone in his cell, reflects on the personal toll of the rebellion. His thoughts reveal a man who is grappling with the harsh realities of his choices.

Sam, in a quiet monologue: "I chose this path, but I never imagined the depth of the sacrifice. The loss... it's overwhelming. Yet, here we stand, unbroken."

The chapter then transitions to a group of young resistance members discussing the ethical implications of their actions. The conversation underscores the complexity of their situation and the moral dilemmas they face.

Young Resistance Member: "We're fighting for freedom, but at times, it feels like we're crossing lines. How far is too far?"

Another Member, thoughtfully: "It's a war, not just of guns, but of ideals. We have to stay true to ours, even when it's hard."

The narrative explores the theme of the greater good versus individual cost. This is illustrated through a series of vignettes depicting the everyday struggles and sacrifices of those in the resistance and the wider community.

In a market, an overheard conversation:

Vendor: "They say it's for our future, but my brother didn't come back from the last raid. Is this the future we want?"

Customer, sympathetically: "It's a heavy price, but maybe it's the price of change. Of a better world for our children."

The chapter concludes with a scene where the main characters gather, their faces reflecting the weariness and resolve that comes with prolonged struggle. They reaffirm their commitment to the cause, acknowledging the costs but also the necessity of their fight.

Ava, rallying the group: "We've all lost something in this fight. But what we're fighting for... it's bigger than any one of us."

Narrative closing: "In the quiet hours of the night, as the city sleeps, the rebels contemplate the cost of their rebellion. In the pursuit of freedom, they find themselves entangled in a web of moral quandaries, each decision a balancing act between sacrifice and hope. Yet, in their hearts, the flame of resistance burns ever bright, a testament to the enduring human spirit in the face of adversity."

This section poignantly captures the internal struggles and the ethical considerations of the resistance, painting a nuanced picture of the complex landscape of rebellion and the moral costs that come with fighting for a deeply held cause.

Personal Growth and Transformation

Protagonist's Evolution

In 'Personal Growth and Transformation,' a crucial part of Chapter 7, 'Reflections and Realizations,' the narrative centers on the protagonist, Sam, and his profound transformation throughout the journey. This section explores how his experiences in the rebellion have shaped his beliefs, sense of self, and worldview, conveyed through introspective dialogues and interactions with other characters.

A significant scene unfolds in Sam's cell, where, in a rare moment of solitude, he reflects on his journey. The dim light of the cell casts shadows that seem to mirror the depth of his thoughts.

Sam, in a quiet soliloquy: "From a bystander to a rebel. I never imagined this path, yet here I am. Each choice, each sacrifice, has chiseled away at who I thought I was, revealing someone stronger, someone... different."

During a covert visit, Maya brings news from the outside, providing a catalyst for Sam to express how he has changed.

Maya, whispering through the cell bars: "You've become a symbol out there, Sam. A beacon of hope."

Sam, with a wry smile: "A symbol, huh? I just wanted to make a difference. But I guess we don't always get to choose how the world sees us."

The narrative then shifts to a flashback, contrasting Sam's initial reluctance to join the resistance with his eventual commitment. This juxtaposition highlights the evolution of his character – from skepticism to unwavering dedication.

Flashback Scene - Sam's First Meeting with the Resistance:

Early Sam, skeptically: "You really think we can change anything? The regime is too powerful."

Ava, from the past, determined: "Every big change starts with a small step. You just have to be brave enough to take it."

Back in the present, Sam's interactions with the resistance members during their visits to his cell reveal his new role as a mentor and strategist, guiding them with wisdom born of his experiences.

During a strategy discussion with Leo, conveyed in hushed tones:

Sam: "Use the regime's arrogance against them. They underestimate us, and that's their biggest weakness."

Leo, acknowledging Sam's growth: "You've come a long way, Sam. Your insights... they're invaluable."

The chapter also touches on how Sam's experiences have altered his perspective on the larger fight against the regime. He sees the struggle not just as a battle for freedom, but as a fight for the soul of the city, a fight that transcends individual desires.

Sam, reflecting aloud to himself: "It's bigger than me, bigger than any of us. It's about shaping the future, about leaving a world worth living in for the next generation."

The section concludes with Sam looking out of his cell window, his gaze fixed on the distant city lights, symbolizing his hope and belief in a better future.

Narrative closing: "In the confines of his cell, Sam embodies the spirit of transformation. His journey from reluctant participant to key strategist and symbol of hope is a testament to the power of personal evolution. In his eyes, reflecting the city's distant lights, lies the unwavering belief that change, though painful, brings forth the promise of a new dawn."

This section poignantly illustrates Sam's profound personal growth and transformation, highlighting how his journey in the rebellion has reshaped his identity and his view of the world.

Relationships and Impact

In 'Personal Growth and Transformation,' Chapter 7 of 'Reflections and Realizations,' a significant focus is placed on how Sam's relationships with fellow resistance members, family, and friends have evolved over the course of his journey. This section delves into the complexities of these relationships, highlighting how they have been impacted by the struggle against the regime and Sam's personal transformation.

A scene unfolds in the resistance's hideout where Ava and Leo discuss Sam and his influence on them and the movement.

Ava, looking at a picture of Sam: "You know, Sam always had a way of making you see things differently. I miss that."

Leo, with a hint of humor: "Yeah, his stubborn optimism. Who would've thought it'd be contagious?"

This dialogue transitions into a flashback of a conversation between Sam and his sister before his imprisonment, emphasizing the personal cost of his involvement in the resistance.

Flashback Scene - Sam and His Sister:

Sam's Sister, concerned: "You're risking everything for this cause. What about us, your family?"

Sam, reassuringly: "I'm doing this for all of us. For a future where we don't have to live in fear."

In the present, Sam reflects on these relationships during his solitary moments in his cell. He grapples with guilt and longing but also a sense of purpose that his fight has brought to his life.

Sam, in a moment of solitude: "I hope they understand why I had to do this. It's not just about me. It's about all of us, our future."

The narrative also touches on the relationships within the resistance. Ava and Leo have grown closer, their bond strengthened by the shared goal and the void left by Sam's absence.

In a quiet moment between Ava and Leo:

Ava: "We've been through so much. Sam brought us together, and now it's up to us to finish what he started."

Leo, looking at Sam's empty seat: "He's still with us, Ava. In every plan we make, every action we take."

As the chapter progresses, the impact of Sam's decisions on his friends outside the resistance is also explored. They grapple with understanding his choices and the dangerous path he has chosen.

In a conversation between two of Sam's old friends:

Friend 1: "Sam was always a dreamer. But I never thought he'd go this far."

Friend 2, with a mix of admiration and concern: "He's fighting for something he believes in. Can't say I'd have the courage to do the same."

The chapter concludes with Sam, alone in his cell, coming to terms with the impact of his decisions on his relationships. He understands that while he has lost much, he has also gained a deeper connection with those who share his vision for a better world.

Narrative closing: "In the quiet reflection of his cell, Sam contemplates the web of relationships that his journey has touched. Each connection, strained or strengthened, tells a story of sacrifice, shared dreams, and the unyielding bonds formed in the crucible of rebellion. For Sam, these relationships are both a reminder of what he's fighting for and a testament to the indelible impact one individual can have in the quest for a better world."

This section poignantly captures the evolution of Sam's relationships throughout his journey, reflecting the personal and interpersonal complexities of participating in a movement much larger than oneself.

Setting the Stage for the Future

Uncertain Outcomes

n 'Personal Growth and Transformation,' a key component of Chapter 7, Reflections and Realizations,' the narrative delves into the theme of uncertain outcomes. Despite some victories by the resistance, the future remains shrouded in ambiguity, with the larger war against the regime continuing to unfold in unforeseen ways.

A pivotal scene unfolds in the resistance's base where Ava, Leo, and other key members discuss their recent successes and the uncertain path ahead.

Ava, scanning recent reports: "We've made some hits, that's for sure. But have we really changed anything yet?"

Leo, leaning over the map: "It's like chopping at a giant tree with a pocket knife. We've made scratches, but the tree still stands."

Their conversation captures the mix of hope and apprehension that defines their situation. They have achieved some tactical wins, but the strategic victory – the fall of the regime – still seems distant.

Maya, joining in: "Every win counts. But yeah, it's hard to see the endgame. Are we making a dent, or just provoking them more?"

In a separate scene, Sam, in his cell, reflects on the broader implications of their struggle. His thoughts reveal a man who understands the complexity of their fight against the regime.

Sam, to himself: "We've lit sparks, sure. But is it enough to ignite a fire? Or are we just flickering in the wind?"

A discussion between some of the younger resistance members brings a different perspective. They are energized by the recent victories but also aware of the long road ahead.

Young Resistance Member: "We're doing something, right? People are talking, fighting back."

Another Young Member, cautiously optimistic: "True, but it's a long fight. The regime isn't just going to roll over and play dead."

Towards the end of the chapter, a key meeting takes place, where the resistance leaders grapple with the uncertainty of their future actions and the impact of their rebellion.

Ava, addressing the group: "We've come far, but the hardest part is still ahead. We don't know what the future holds, but we have to be ready for anything."

Leo, with a mix of determination and humor: "Well, uncertainty keeps life interesting, right? Just wish it wasn't quite this interesting."

The chapter concludes with a scene of Sam, once again alone in his cell, his gaze fixed on the tiny window that offers a sliver of the outside world. His expression is thoughtful, a blend of determination and the weariness of a man who has seen too much yet still dares to hope.

Narrative closing: "In the quiet confines of his cell, Sam stares into the night, his thoughts a mirror of the resistance's. The future is a canvas of uncertainties, each stroke of rebellion painting a picture of hope and fear, victory and loss. The road ahead is shrouded in mist, but the journey continues, step by uncertain step, towards a future only time will reveal."

This section of the chapter emphasizes the theme of uncertainty in the ongoing struggle against the regime. It captures the complexities and ambiguities inherent in any rebellion, leaving the reader with a sense of anticipation and reflection on the unpredictable nature of such a fight.

Hints of Hope and Despair

In 'Setting the Stage for the Future,' the final section of Chapter 7, 'Reflections and Realizations,' the narrative artfully balances the interplay of hope and despair as it lays the groundwork for what lies ahead. This part of the story captures the dichotomy of a world in flux, where positive changes in some areas are shadowed by deepening chaos in others.

The chapter opens with Ava and Leo observing the city from a hidden vantage point, reflecting on the changes they've witnessed.

Ava, looking out at the city: "Some parts of the city are waking up, fighting back. There's hope there."

Leo, with a hint of cynicism: "And then there's the West District. It's like a scene from a dystopian movie, only the popcorn's missing."

This observation leads to a broader discussion about the uneven nature of the rebellion's impact.

In a strategy meeting with other resistance leaders:

Resistance Leader: "In some neighborhoods, we're seeing real change. People are standing up."

Another Leader, more somber: "But in others, fear's gripping tighter than ever. The regime's making sure of that."

The narrative shifts to show scenes from different parts of the city. In one district, graffiti celebrating the resistance adorns the walls, while in another, regime propaganda posters are plastered over every surface, and citizens move in fear.

In a bustling market square, a vendor mutters to a customer:

Vendor: "You hear about the East Side? They're organizing, taking a stand."

Customer, glancing nervously around: "Wish we could do that here. But you know how it is... too many eyes."

Sam, in his cell, has a moment of contemplation. Despite his confinement, he remains attuned to the changing tides outside.

Sam, reflecting to himself: "Change is like the tide, I guess. It comes in waves, some parts rising before others."

The chapter concludes with a scene of a secret meeting where the resistance plans their next move. The atmosphere is a mix of determination and apprehension.

Ava, addressing the group: "We're making progress, but let's not kid ourselves. This is a long game, and it's going to get tougher."

Leo, injecting a bit of dark humor: "So, business as usual then? I was starting to get bored with all the peace and quiet."

Narrative closing: "As the chapter closes on a world of contrasts, the resistance faces the duality of their struggle. In the shadows of hope, despair lingers, a reminder of the complex battle they wage. Yet, amid the uncertainty and fear, the flickers of change ignite a fire of resilience, casting light on the path ahead. The stage is set, not for an end, but for a new beginning, where every act of defiance, every whisper of hope, contributes to the unfolding story of a world in search of freedom."

This section of the chapter skillfully sets the stage for future developments in the story, highlighting the complex interplay of hope and despair in a world caught between the throes of rebellion and the grip of an oppressive regime.

End with Open Questions

In 'Setting the Stage for the Future,' the concluding section of Chapter 7, 'Reflections and Realizations,' the narrative skillfully leaves the reader pondering a series of open questions and unresolved issues. This section amplifies the intrigue and uncertainty about the future of the protagonist, the resistance, and the world at large, setting a tone of suspense and contemplation.

The chapter culminates in a reflective scene where Ava and Leo, in the dim light of their hideout, ponder the unknowns of their situation.

Ava, with a contemplative gaze: "Do you ever wonder if we'll see the end of this? If our fight will actually change anything?"

Leo, leaning against a wall: "Every day. But then I remember Sam stuck in that cell, and I think, we don't really have a choice, do we?"

In a separate moment, the narrative shifts to Sam in his cell, where he too grapples with questions about his fate and the broader implications of their struggle.

Sam, speaking softly to himself: "What's my role in all this now? A strategist from a cell, a symbol... but what else? Will I ever walk the streets of a free city?"

As the chapter draws to a close, a clandestine meeting of the resistance leaders takes place, underscoring the uncertainty about the movement's future.

During the meeting:

Young Resistance Member: "What happens next? Do we keep fighting like this forever?"

Maya, with a determined yet uncertain tone: "We keep going until something gives. We're writing history here, even if we don't know the ending yet."

The scene transitions to a quiet street at night, where citizens whisper about the resistance's actions and their possible consequences.

Citizen 1, in a hushed tone: "They say the resistance is planning something big. Will it be enough?"

Citizen 2, skeptically: "Who knows? But I'd rather cling to a shred of hope than accept this as our fate."

The chapter ends with an aerial view of the city, its lights flickering like stars, symbolizing both the hope and the lingering darkness that envelop the narrative.

Narrative closing: "As the curtain falls on this chapter, the city rests under a blanket of unanswered questions and uncharted futures. The fate of Sam, the destiny of the resistance, and the course of the world remain suspended in the balance, like stars waiting to chart their course in the night sky. In this world of shadows and light, every choice, every action, resonates with the possibility of change, leaving the reader to wonder: what comes next?"

This ending effectively leaves the story open-ended, inviting the reader to ponder the multitude of possibilities and scenarios that could unfold in the ongoing battle for freedom and justice in a world marked by both hope and despair.

Epilogue: Beyond the Horizon

A Look into the Future

Temporal Leap

In the Epilogue, titled 'Beyond the Horizon,' the narrative takes a bold leap forward in time, providing a glimpse into how the world has evolved in the years following the tumultuous events of the main narrative. This temporal jump, spanning several years, paints a picture of a world still grappling with the legacy of the past but moving towards an uncertain future.

The epilogue opens in a bustling city square, markedly different from the oppressive atmosphere depicted in earlier chapters. The scene is set a decade after the events of the main narrative. Citizens move freely, the air is filled with a sense of cautious optimism.

A street artist, speaking to a group of onlookers: "Can you believe it's been ten years since the regime fell? Feels like yesterday and a lifetime ago, all at once."

One of the onlookers, a young woman who grew up during the rebellion: "I was just a kid then, but I remember. It's strange to think how much has changed."

The narrative then transitions to a commemorative event, where former resistance members, including Ava and Leo, gather to honor those lost in the struggle and to reflect on the journey.

Ava, addressing the crowd: "We've come a long way since those dark days. The world we fought for... it's not perfect, but it's ours. And it was worth every sacrifice."

Leo, with his characteristic dry humor: "Yeah, who knew we'd actually pull it off? Guess we're not just a bunch of troublemakers after all."

In this future, the resistance has transformed into a movement for rebuilding and healing. The focus has shifted from overthrowing a regime to fostering a society based on the ideals they fought for.

At a roundtable discussion, a former resistance strategist now turned community leader says: "Our battle was not just against a regime, but for a vision of society. Now, we have the chance to build it."

The epilogue also hints at lingering challenges and the enduring scars left by the past. Despite the fall of the regime, the path to true freedom and equality is still fraught with obstacles.

In a quiet café, two elderly citizens converse:

Elderly Citizen 1: "They did it, they actually did it. But the road ahead is still long and winding."

Elderly Citizen 2, nodding: "True, but at least now there's hope. A chance to make things right for the coming generations."

As the epilogue draws to a close, a scene is set in a small, peaceful park where a statue of Sam stands as a symbol of the enduring spirit of resistance and the power of the individual to spark change.

A mother, explaining to her child: "That man there, he helped change our world. He showed us that even in the darkest times, one voice can light up the sky."

Narrative closing: "As the sun sets on a city reborn from the ashes of its tumultuous past, the legacy of the rebellion lives on in every street, every building, and every heart. The journey from darkness to light is never easy, but as the people of this world look towards the horizon, they do so with eyes full of hope, knowing that the future is theirs to shape."

This temporal leap in the epilogue serves as a powerful conclusion to the narrative, offering a hopeful yet realistic view of a world forever changed by the events and sacrifices of the past, and a reminder that the journey towards a better future is ongoing and ever-evolving.

Global Landscape

The 'A Look into the Future' section of 'Beyond the Horizon,' the epilogue of the novel, vividly paints the global landscape in the years following the main narrative. This part explores the aftermath of the resistance's efforts, revealing a world that has experienced significant changes in some regions, while others remain under the shadow of oppressive regimes.

The epilogue begins with an overview of the global scene, depicted through a series of interconnected vignettes from various parts of the world.

In a bustling European city square, two tourists discuss the changes:

Tourist 1, looking at a news display: "Looks like the Eastern Bloc is finally breaking free from the regime's clutches. It's been a long fight."

Tourist 2, with a hint of irony: "Yeah, and just when you thought the world couldn't get any crazier. Next thing you know, we'll have flying cars."

In another part of the world, a scene unfolds in a South American village where the regime's influence is still strongly felt. The contrast is stark, underscoring the uneven nature of change.

In the village, a local activist speaks to a small group: "We've seen the North rise up and make strides, but here, we're still fighting for the basics. It's our turn now."

The narrative then shifts to Asia, where a mix of progress and ongoing struggles paints a complex picture.

In a bustling Asian metropolis, a group of young activists gather in a café:

Young Activist: "The regime's grip is loosening, but it's not gone. We've got to keep pushing, keep the momentum."

Her friend, sipping tea: "One step at a time. Remember, a journey of a thousand miles and all that."

Throughout these scenes, the narrative highlights the interconnectedness of the global struggle against oppression. While some regions celebrate their newfound freedoms, others continue to fight against the remnants of the regime.

The epilogue also provides a glimpse into the advancements and setbacks in technology, economy, and human rights that have occurred in different parts of the world.

In an international conference, a delegate speaks:

Delegate: "In some places, technology has liberated us, but elsewhere, it's become another tool of control. The global landscape is a patchwork of progress and challenges."

As the epilogue draws to a close, a sense of global solidarity emerges, with a recognition that the fight for freedom and justice is a shared human endeavor.

Narrative closing: "As the world turns, the tapestry of the global landscape reveals itself to be a mosaic of change – vibrant patches of liberation interwoven with threads of ongoing struggle. From the sprawling cities to the quiet villages, the echoes of the resistance resonate, a reminder that while the battle may be local, the war is universal. In this ever-changing world, the only constant is the enduring spirit of humanity, forever striving towards a horizon of hope and equality."

This section of the epilogue effectively sets the stage for a world that is both changed and unchanged, reflecting the complex and ongoing nature of the struggle against tyranny and the universal quest for freedom and dignity.

The Protagonist's Legacy

Reflections on the Protagonist's Legacy

In 'The Protagonist's Legacy,' a pivotal section of the Epilogue, 'Beyond the Horizon,' the narrative delves into the enduring impact of Sam, the protagonist. Whether he remains active in the resistance, has become a symbol, or has passed away, his legacy is explored through reflections and dialogues, showcasing how he has left an indelible mark on the world and the resistance movement.

The section opens in a small, cozy classroom where a history teacher discusses recent events with her students.

Teacher, addressing the class: "And then there was Sam, a key figure in the resistance. His actions sparked a wave of change that reshaped our world."

Student, curiously: "Is it true he planned rebellions from his prison cell?"

Teacher, with a smile: "That's what the stories say. Whether myth or fact, he's become a symbol of our fight for freedom."

The narrative then transitions to a gathering of former resistance members, where they reminisce about Sam and his contributions.

In a dimly lit café, Ava and Leo share a quiet conversation:

Ava, raising her cup: "To Sam, who showed us the power of a single voice against the darkness."

Leo, with his usual dry wit: "Yeah, he had a knack for trouble. But he turned it into an art form."

In another scene, a museum dedicated to the resistance movement features an exhibit on Sam, highlighting his role and the sacrifices he made.

A tour guide, speaking to a group of visitors: "This section is dedicated to Sam. His story is one of courage and resilience, a testament to the human spirit's capacity for change."

Visitor, looking at a photo of Sam: "It's incredible, one person can make such a difference."

The narrative also touches on the personal side of Sam, reflecting on his relationships and how they influenced his actions.

In a quiet park, Sam's sister speaks to her own child about him:

Sister, pointing to a statue of Sam: "That's your uncle. He fought so that we could live in a better world. He always said, 'Our choices define us.'"

Child, wide-eyed: "He must've been really brave."

As the epilogue draws to a close, a scene unfolds at a memorial for the resistance, where Sam's name is etched alongside others who fought for freedom.

Ava, standing by the memorial: "They say you die twice. Once when you stop breathing, and once when somebody says your name for the last time. Looks like Sam's going to live forever."

Narrative closing: "In the annals of history and the hearts of those who dream of a freer world, Sam's legacy endures. From whispered stories in classrooms to solemn memorials, his spirit lives on, a beacon guiding those who continue the fight. In a world forever changed, Sam remains a symbol of hope, courage, and the unyielding pursuit of justice."

This section of the epilogue poignantly reflects on the protagonist's lasting legacy, showcasing how his actions and choices have rippled through time, inspiring generations and leaving an indelible mark on the fabric of society and the ongoing struggle for freedom.

Influence on New Generations

In the 'The Protagonist's Legacy' section of the Epilogue, 'Beyond the Horizon,' the narrative shifts focus to illustrate the profound influence of Sam, the protagonist, on new generations. It showcases how his actions, ideals, and sacrifices have inspired and shaped the minds and paths of young characters and how others continue to carry the torch of his work.

The section opens in a bustling urban school, where a group of teenagers gather around a holographic exhibit featuring Sam's life and his role in the resistance.

Teen 1, with a touch of awe: "Look at this! Sam was like a superhero, but real. Fighting from the shadows, outsmarting the regime."

Teen 2, half-jokingly: "Yeah, with no cape or superpowers. Just guts and a lot of stubbornness."

The narrative then shifts to a youth group meeting where young activists discuss strategies and ideas for social change, drawing inspiration from Sam's story.

At the meeting, a young activist speaks passionately: "Sam's story proves one thing – you don't need to be a legend to make a difference. It's about standing up for what's right, even if you stand alone at first."

Another young activist, thoughtfully: "It's not just about fighting against something, but building something new. That's the real challenge."

In a heartwarming scene, an elderly Leo is seen speaking to a group of young volunteers at a community center that was established in honor of the resistance's efforts.

Leo, sharing his experiences: "Sam always said, 'Change starts with an idea, a spark.' You all are that spark for a new generation."

A young volunteer, inspired: "We're ready to carry that spark forward. Sam's story won't end with him. It's just the beginning."

The narrative also explores how Sam's ideals have been integrated into the fabric of the society, influencing policies, educational programs, and cultural narratives.

In a local council meeting, a councilor reflects: "Our approach to governance, to treating each other with dignity and respect, it's a legacy of those who fought for change, like Sam."

The chapter concludes with a scene set in a peaceful park, where a statue of Sam stands. A child, accompanied by their parent, looks up at the statue in wonder.

Child, curiously: "Who was he?"

Parent, smiling: "Someone who believed in a better world and fought to make it happen. Now, it's up to us to keep that dream alive."

Narrative closing: "As the sun sets on a world still writing its story, the echo of Sam's legacy resonates through the streets, in classrooms, council halls, and the hearts of those who dare to dream. His spirit, embodied in the aspirations and actions of new generations, continues to inspire a relentless pursuit of a just and free world. In the annals of history, Sam's influence transcends time, igniting the flames of change in every young mind that believes in the power of one to alter the course of many."

This section of the epilogue effectively showcases the enduring impact of the protagonist on future generations, depicting how his ideals, courage, and actions continue to inspire and shape a world that is still in the process of healing and growing from its tumultuous past.

Ongoing Struggles and New Challenges

Persistent Issues

In the 'Ongoing Struggles and New Challenges' section of the Epilogue, 'Beyond the Horizon,' the narrative acknowledges that despite significant victories, the war against oppression and for freedom is an ongoing endeavor. This part of the story delves into the new challenges emerging in the persistent fight against authoritarianism, painting a picture of a world still grappling with complex issues.

The section begins in a bustling media center, where journalists discuss the current state of global politics and the enduring issues of authoritarianism.

Journalist 1, scanning the latest headlines: "Looks like the Northern Coalition is facing a new authoritarian wave. The more things change, huh?"

Journalist 2, with a cynical chuckle: "Yeah, freedom's a tricky business. One minute you're celebrating victory, the next you're back in the trenches."

In another part of the world, a scene unfolds in a town hall meeting where citizens express their concerns about the resurgence of oppressive tactics by local authorities.

Concerned Citizen, speaking out: "We thought we were past this. New faces, same old tactics. Surveillance, censorship... it's like a bad rerun."

Town Hall Speaker, trying to rally the crowd: "We've faced this before, and we'll face it again. It's our right to stand up, to keep the spirit of the resistance alive."

The narrative shifts to a university, where a group of students debate the complexities of maintaining freedom in a world where authoritarianism constantly evolves.

Student Debater: "The problem is, authoritarianism is like a shape-shifter. Knock it down in one place, and it pops up in another."

Another Student, thoughtfully: "True, but that just means our fight has to be just as adaptable. Keep evolving, just like they do."

In a poignant scene, a family gathers around the dinner table, discussing the importance of remaining vigilant in the face of new threats to their freedom.

Parent, addressing their children: "Remember, freedom isn't a one-time victory. It's a garden that needs constant tending."

Teenage Child, with a mix of idealism and sarcasm: "Great, so we're gardening now? I thought this was about fighting the power."

As the epilogue draws to a close, a vigil is held in a city square, where people light candles in memory of those lost and in solidarity against the resurgence of oppressive forces.

Ava, now an elder, speaks to the crowd: "Our journey isn't over. The road to freedom is long and winding, but as long as we walk it together, we keep the hope alive."

Narrative closing: "As night falls on a world still finding its way, the flickering candles in the square cast a soft glow, a testament to the undying human spirit. In this ever-changing landscape, the battles may shift, and new challenges arise, but the quest for freedom and justice endures, a beacon for generations to come. In the echo of their voices, in the strength of their resolve, the story continues – a story of persistence, resilience, and the unyielding fight for a brighter tomorrow."

This section of the epilogue paints a realistic picture of a world in continuous flux, where victories in the struggle for freedom and democracy are interspersed with new challenges and the enduring need for vigilance and resilience.

Evolving Resistance

In 'Ongoing Struggles and New Challenges,' a crucial segment of 'Beyond the Horizon,' the Epilogue of the novel, the focus shifts to how the resistance has transformed and adapted to the changing global landscape. This part of the story explores the evolution of the resistance, examining whether they have become more organized, or fragmented into different factions with varying ideologies.

The section begins in a revamped resistance headquarters, now operating more like a coordinated movement center. Ava, still a key figure in the resistance, is seen leading a strategy meeting.

Ava, addressing the room: "The world's changed, and so have we. We're not just rebels in the shadows anymore; we're a movement with a voice."

Young Activist, somewhat skeptically: "Sure, but are we singing the same tune? Last I checked, the East Faction had some pretty radical ideas."

This introduces the concept of ideological differences within the resistance. As the movement has grown, so have the divergent paths and strategies within it.

In another scene, two factions of the resistance engage in a heated debate over their future direction.

East Faction Leader: "We need direct action, hit them where it hurts. Show we mean business."

West Faction Representative, cautioning: "And risk everything we've built? We need a more diplomatic approach now."

The narrative then shifts to a grassroots community meeting, where local resistance members discuss the importance of maintaining unity despite their differences.

Community Leader, passionately: "We can't let our differences divide us. We're stronger together, remember?"

Local Activist, with a hint of humor: "Yeah, united we stand, divided we fall. Or at least trip over each other a lot."

In a poignant moment, the story reveals how some members of the original resistance have chosen to step back from active involvement, focusing instead on education and community building.

In a casual conversation between former resistance members:

Former Member: "I've hung up my protest boots. These days, I'm teaching the next generation about what we fought for."

Friend, with a playful smirk: "So, from dodging tear gas to grading papers. Quite the career change."

As the epilogue draws to a close, a scene is set in a public square where a statue of Sam stands as a reminder of the resistance's roots. A group of young people gather around it, discussing their role in the evolving resistance.

Young Person, looking up at the statue: "Sam started something big, but it's up to us to keep it going, in whatever way we can."

Their Friend, optimistically: "Yeah, whether that's in the streets, in the halls of power, or somewhere in between."

Narrative closing: "As the sun sets on a world still in the throes of change, the legacy of the resistance lives on, morphed and multiplied into a myriad of voices, each singing their own version of freedom's song. In the shadow of Sam's statue, a new generation gathers, ready to write their chapter in the ongoing saga of the fight for justice. The resistance, ever-evolving, continues to adapt and grow, as diverse and dynamic as the world it seeks to change."

This section of the epilogue offers a vivid portrayal of the resistance's evolution, capturing the complexities and challenges of maintaining a unified front in a world where the fight for freedom and justice takes many forms.

Enduring Themes and Questions

Philosophical Contemplation

In 'Enduring Themes and Questions,' the final section of the Epilogue 'Beyond the Horizon,' the narrative culminates in a profound philosophical contemplation on the central themes of the book: freedom, control, surveillance, and the balance between individual and collective good. This contemplation is woven through dialogues and monologues, capturing the essence of the novel's overarching message.

The scene opens in a university classroom where a professor leads a thought-provoking discussion with students about the book's themes.

Professor, engaging the class: "Let's consider the themes we've encountered – freedom, control, the ever-watchful eye of surveillance. How do they resonate in our world today?"

Student 1, ponderously: "Freedom's a tricky beast. We fought for it, but maintaining it... that's a whole other battle."

Student 2, with a hint of irony: "And don't forget about control. It's like playing whack-a-mole – knock it down in one place, and it pops up in another."

In another scene, a group of activists gathers in a park, reflecting on the balance between individual rights and the collective good.

Activist 1, thoughtfully: "It's a fine line, isn't it? Push too hard for individual rights, and you might trample on the collective good."

Activist 2, with a smirk: "Yeah, but lean too much on the collective, and next thing you know, you're back under someone's boot. It's all about balance, I guess."

A poignant moment unfolds in a memorial dedicated to those who fought against oppression, where visitors contemplate the cost of freedom and the vigilance required to preserve it.

Visitor, reading the inscriptions: "It's amazing what they sacrificed for freedom. Makes you wonder, how far would you go to protect it?"

Companion, reflectively: "And not just protect, but nurture it. Freedom's like a plant – ignore it, and it withers away."

Towards the end of the epilogue, an elderly couple sit on a bench, watching the sunset, musing on the changes they've witnessed over the years.

Elderly Man: "We've seen so much, haven't we? The rise and fall of regimes, the dance of freedom and control."

Elderly Woman, nodding: "True. And yet, the questions remain. How do we balance safety and freedom? Surveillance and privacy? The debates of our youth are still the debates of today."

The epilogue concludes with a narrative reflection, tying together these contemplations and leaving the reader with enduring questions to ponder.

Narrative closing: "As the sun dips below the horizon, casting long shadows across a world still grappling with age-old questions, the themes of freedom, control, surveillance, and the delicate dance between individual and collective good continue to resonate. In the echoes of these philosophical musings, the story finds its true heart – not in the answers, but in the relentless pursuit of the questions, in the unending quest to understand, to challenge, and to balance the complexities of a world ever in flux. In this quest, the legacy of the book lives on, a timeless reflection on the human condition and our perpetual struggle to find harmony in a world of contradictions."

This section of the epilogue offers a deep and thoughtful contemplation of the enduring themes presented in the book, inviting readers to continue engaging with the critical questions that define our collective journey towards understanding freedom, control, and the balance between individuality and the greater good.

Unanswered Questions

In 'Enduring Themes and Questions,' the closing section of the Epilogue 'Beyond the Horizon,' the narrative artfully leaves certain questions unanswered or open-ended. This approach encourages readers to ponder the possibilities and form their own conclusions about the critical and thought-provoking issues raised throughout the novel.

The section opens with a group of characters gathered in a café, engaged in a lively debate about the unresolved aspects of the story.

Character 1, with a puzzled expression: "But what about the fate of the digital surveillance network? Did they dismantle it, or did it just evolve into something else?"

Character 2, shrugging: "Guess that's for us to figure out. Maybe it's a case of 'watch this space'... literally."

In another scene, a teacher uses the open-ended nature of the story to spark a discussion among her students about the future implications of the themes presented in the book.

Teacher, encouraging debate: "So, what do you think happens next? How do these themes play out in our world, in the future?"

Student, thoughtfully: "It's like the author left us a puzzle. We've got the pieces, but it's up to us to put them together."

The narrative then shifts to a public forum, where citizens discuss the broader implications of the story for their society and the ongoing struggle for freedom and justice.

Citizen 1, in a public debate: "The story ends, but the questions it raises, they're still very much alive. How do we balance freedom and security, privacy and transparency?"

Citizen 2, humorously: "And the biggest question: will we ever get politicians to read this book and actually learn something?"

In the final scene, a group of old friends who were part of the resistance reminisce about their experiences and ponder the future.

Old Friend 1, nostalgically: "We did what we could, but the story's far from over. The next chapters... well, they're for the next generation to write."

Old Friend 2, with a smirk: "Just hope they write it better than some of our plans. Remember the 'great distraction' fiasco?"

As the epilogue concludes, the narrative voice chimes in, leaving readers with a sense of continuity and the enduring relevance of the story's themes.

Narrative closing: "As the characters' voices fade into the background, the questions they leave hanging in the air linger like a haunting melody. These unanswered questions, like open doors to infinite possibilities, invite the reader to step through, to explore, and to continue the dialogue. In the spaces between the words, the story lives on, an ever-evolving tapestry of thought and imagination, challenging each reader to question, to ponder, and to dream of what lies beyond the horizon."

This section of the epilogue masterfully leaves the door open for readers to engage with the narrative beyond the confines of the book, encouraging a continued exploration of its themes and questions in the context of their own lives and societies.

Final Vignettes

Snapshots of the World

In 'Final Vignettes,' the concluding section of the Epilogue 'Beyond the Horizon,' the narrative offers a mosaic of brief vignettes, each providing a snapshot of life in various parts of the world. These scenes collectively illustrate how different societies and individuals have adapted to or continue to grapple with the changes and ongoing struggles in a post-rebellion era.

1. **A bustling street market in Southeast Asia:** Vendors call out their wares while a group of teenagers gather around a graffiti mural depicting scenes from the resistance.

Teenager 1, proudly: "My grandpa was part of that. Says it was rough, but worth it."

Teenager 2, jokingly: "And now we complain when the net's down for ten minutes. We're definitely the cushy generation."

2. **A high-tech boardroom in Europe:** Business leaders discuss the integration of ethical AI in governance, with a hologram of Sam in the background.

CEO, with a half-smile: "Remember when AI was the big bad wolf? Now it's like our pet dog, keeping us on the ethical straight and narrow."

Board Member, chuckling: "Just hope it doesn't start giving us commands. I'm not ready for robot overlords just yet."

3. **A classroom in North America:** A teacher concludes a lesson on recent history, focusing on the global shift towards more democratic practices.

Teacher, closing the book: "And that's how people power reshaped our world. Any questions?"

Student, curiously: "Do you think we'll ever have to fight like that again?"

Teacher, thoughtfully: "History has a way of repeating itself, but it's up to us to write a different ending."

4. **A rural village in Africa:** A community meeting under a large tree, where elders and youth discuss sustainable development.

Elder, wisely: "We've seen the world change, but we keep our traditions. Respect for the earth, for each other – that's our way."

Young Villager, earnestly: "And with the new tech, we can make it even better. Tradition and progress, hand in hand."

5. **A quiet café in South America:** Former resistance members gather, sharing stories and memories.

Former Rebel, nostalgically: "Those were the days, huh? Dodging surveillance drones, hacking into broadcasts..."

Companion, laughing: "And now what? We fight over the best coffee beans. Times change, amigo."

6. **A peaceful park in the Middle East:** Families enjoy an afternoon outdoors, where children play freely, a stark contrast to the regime's past oppression.

Parent, watching the children: "They'll grow up without fear. That's the real victory."

Friend, smiling: "Yeah, a world where the biggest worry is a scraped knee. We've come a long way."

Narrative closing: "As these vignettes fade, they leave behind a tapestry rich with the hues of change, resilience, and hope. From bustling markets to tranquil parks, the world spins on, each scene a testament to the enduring human spirit. In the laughter of children, the wisdom of elders, and the passion of youth, the legacy of the past melds with the promise of the future, painting a picture of a world forever changed, yet still evolving. In these final snapshots, the story finds its resting place, not in the closure, but in the continuous rhythm of life — a rhythm that beats to the drum of freedom, adaptation, and enduring hope."

These final vignettes in the epilogue serve as a panoramic view of a world reshaped by its past struggles and triumphs, offering glimpses into diverse societies and individual lives as they navigate the complexities of a post-rebellion era. Each snapshot captures the essence of a world that is both marked by its history and looking forward to the future.

Closing Thoughts

In 'Final Vignettes,' the last segment of the Epilogue 'Beyond the Horizon,' the narrative culminates with a poignant closing thought. This statement is designed to encapsulate the spirit of the novel, leaving a lasting and reflective impression on the reader, tying together the themes of freedom, struggle, and hope in a world rife with challenges and change.

The scene is set on a quiet rooftop in a city that once was a battleground of ideologies. A small group of diverse individuals, young and old, gather under the stars, reflecting on the journey that has been and the path that lies ahead.

Older Member, looking at the stars: "You know, the night sky hasn't changed much since our days of rebellion. Same stars, same moon. But down here, it's a whole new world."

Younger Member, with a hint of wonder: "And to think, it all started with a few brave souls who dared to dream of change."

They fall into a reflective silence, each lost in their thoughts, until a middle-aged woman, who had been a young activist during the rebellion, speaks up.

Middle-Aged Woman: "I used to think freedom was a destination, you know? A place we'd all arrive at one day and just... relax. But I've learned it's more like a journey. Never-ending, always evolving."

Teenager, playfully: "So, no retirement plans for freedom fighters, huh?"

Middle-Aged Woman, with a soft chuckle: "Afraid not. It's a lifelong gig. But one worth every step."

As the night deepens, a final voice chimes in, that of a seasoned writer who had chronicled the rebellion and its aftermath.

Writer, pensively: "In the end, it's not just the battles we won or lost that define us. It's the courage to fight them, the strength to keep going, and the hope that someday, somehow, things will be better."

Narrative closing: "As their voices fade into the quiet night, the story too finds its rest, not in a grand finale, but in the gentle reassurance of continuous struggle and hope. The stars above, timeless and unchanging, bear witness to the ever-evolving saga below – a saga of brave hearts and restless spirits, each playing their part in the grand tapestry of time. And in this quiet moment of reflection under the celestial canopy, the spirit of the novel breathes its essence – a testament to the enduring power of hope, the resilience of the human spirit, and the unyielding pursuit of freedom. In the echoes of this closing thought, the story lingers, a gentle reminder that in every heart lies the capacity to challenge the darkness, to seek the light, and to forever alter the course of history."

This closing thought in the epilogue encapsulates the essence of the novel, leaving readers with a sense of continuity and hope, and the understanding that the struggle for a better world is an ongoing journey, filled with challenges but also with the unbreakable spirit of resilience and hope.

Remember, in the relentless march of time, each step we take shapes our future. Stand firm, be the beacon in the darkness, and never yield to the whims of those who would steer our world into chaos. Our strength lies in our unity, our courage, and our unwavering resolve to forge a path of freedom and truth. Let us walk together, undaunted, in the light of our convictions, and remind the world that the power of the many will always outshine the plans of the few.

Alan E Shields

Inspired by George Orwell

Printed in Great Britain
by Amazon

35713319R00101